Black Velvet

The Erin O'Reilly Mysteries
Book One

Steven Henry

Clickworks Press • Baltimore, MD

First publication: Clickworks Press, 2017
Release: CP-EOR1-INT-P.IS-1.2

Sign up for updates, deals, and exclusive sneak peeks
at clickworkspress.com/join.

ISBN-10: 1-943383-35-9
ISBN-13: 978-1-943383-35-1

For Ingrid, my inspiration

Black Velvet

Fill a glass halfway with champagne. Pour chilled stout beer over an upside-down spoon to fill the flute the rest of the way. This causes the stout to run down the sides of the glass, resulting in a layered drink.

Chapter 1

"We have a ten-thirty-one at 82-37 164th Street. Nearest unit, respond."

Officer Erin O'Reilly punched the radio button. "Sixteen Charlie responding, ten-four. ETA three minutes."

"Ten-four, Sixteen Charlie," Dispatch replied. "Backup units inbound, seven minutes."

Erin turned onto Grand Central Parkway and sped up. "No siren," she said to her partner. "Don't want the bastards to know we're coming."

Rolf didn't disagree. He stared out the window of the squad car, waiting patiently. He was the best partner Erin had ever worked with. He never complained, never made the usual squad-room comments about female cops. He was totally reliable and entirely fearless. His focus on the job was incredible; he ate it, breathed it, lived it. He'd spent his childhood in Bavaria, and his first language was German, but he'd learned enough English to do his job.

Rolf was extraordinary. Erin had worked with him for almost eighteen months, and as far as she was concerned, she never wanted or needed another partner. He was a German

Shepherd, but that just meant she could sleep with him without causing gossip at the precinct.

She steered her Dodge Charger onto 164th northbound. "Dispatch, what's the target building?" she asked.

There was a short pause. "It's a discount uniform store," came the reply.

"Uniforms?" Erin wondered. It sounded like a Halloween prank, but this was early June. It was probably just junkies breaking into the till, looking for a little cash for their next fix.

The time was just after two in the morning, and traffic was light. Erin eased up and braked carefully, not wanting to alert the perps with a squeal of tires. She pulled into a parking space just short of the strip of stores that contained the target building. Putting the car in park, she took a moment to plan her next move.

A 10-31 was a burglary in progress. Protocol dictated that she wait for backup, but according to Dispatch, the other cars were still several minutes out. The perps would be long gone by the time reinforcements arrived. She narrowed her eyes and examined the storefront. There was a broken pane of glass in one of the display windows. That constituted probable cause. She could legally enter.

"Okay, Rolf," she said. "Let's do this." Hitting the radio button once more, she said, "Sixteen Charlie on scene. Signs of forced entry. Engaging." She opened her door and stepped out onto the street.

The first thing she did was draw her Glock. Then she hit the quick-release on Rolf's compartment. Ninety pounds of Shepherd hit the pavement, eager for action. The dog's ears were perked, his nose thrust forward and quivering with excitement.

There was a car parked in front of the store, and she hadn't seen that it was occupied. Its engine coughed to life. It peeled out, laying rubber on the blacktop. She panned her flashlight over the escaping car, catching the license plate in the beam. Then she flicked her radio. "Dispatch, suspect vehicle northbound on 164th, silver Corolla, plate Robert David Adam six three niner niner," she snapped. She couldn't be in two places at once, and she had to secure the crime scene. Besides, with the other car's head start, she'd probably lose them.

There was nothing to do but keep moving forward. She approached the darkened store, pistol ready. "NYPD!" she shouted. "Come out with your hands in the air! I have a canine here. If you don't come out in fifteen seconds, I will send him in, and he *will* bite you."

It was impressive how effective a police threat was when backed up by teeth. A drunken thug might think he could fight half a dozen police officers, but put him up against a dog like Rolf and he'd fold like an accordion. Erin figured there was something primal in people that made them more afraid of fangs than of bullets.

This time, however, there was no answer. "Okay, Rolf," she said, using the German command he'd been trained with. "*Such.*"

The dog went through the broken window in a single leap. Erin drew her flashlight into her off-hand and switched it on. She followed close on Rolf's heels. He was fast and nimble, and wearing a dog-fitted bulletproof vest, but she wasn't about to let her partner face trouble without backup.

The flashlight beam illuminated racks of shirts and trousers. The clothes cast human-like shadows against the walls of the darkened store, making Erin's nerves twitch. But Rolf's nose wasn't fooled. He went straight for the counter at the back of the room. He barked once, sharply, which told Erin everything she needed to know. Someone was hiding behind the counter.

"Come out!" she shouted. She walked carefully, her feet crossing over each other, broken glass crunching under her shoes. She held her wrists crossed, lower hand directing the flashlight, upper hand aiming the Glock. "This is your last warning!"

She paused one more moment. Nothing moved. "Have it your way. Rolf, *fass!*"

The Shepherd snarled and lunged out of sight behind the wood paneling.

"Jesus Christ!" a young and very frightened voice screamed. "Help! Get it off me!"

Rolf's enthusiastic growls accompanied the cries. Erin stepped quickly to the counter and peered around it, keeping her pistol and light trained.

She had to smile at the sight as the tension drained out of her. A young man, more of a kid really, lay on his back, arms crossed to protect his face. Rolf had seized his right arm and held it tightly between his jaws. The kid was a young punk in a leather jacket too big for him, butt-dragging jeans, and a pair of ratty sneakers. He didn't look the least bit threatening. All the same, a New York patrol officer learned not to make assumptions. For all she knew, the kid had a gun in his pocket.

"*Pust!*" Erin said. True to his training, Rolf released the kid but didn't step back. He continued straddling the boy, hackles straining against the collar of his vest, a low growl rumbling in his throat. His tail lashed from side to side, but it was excitement, not friendliness.

She took in the scene, the cash register with its drawer jimmied, the flathead screwdriver on the floor, the scattered dollar bills. "On your stomach," she ordered.

"Crazy dog bit me!" the kid protested. "I'm bleeding, man!"

"I *told* you he would," Erin said. She kept her gun trained on him. "You'll live. Next time, when a cop tells you to come out, you come out. On your belly. Now." Still protesting, he rolled over.

"Hands behind your back," she said, planting a knee in his back, holstering her Glock, and pulling out her cuffs. She snapped them on his wrists with a quick, easy movement. "Decided to do a little late-night shopping, huh? Thought you'd just help yourself to the register?"

"I don't know what you're talking about," he said sullenly.

"Look, kid," she said, bending close to speak into his ear. "I've got you at the scene of a burglary in progress. I've got you for forced entry, and if your fingerprints are on that screwdriver, I've got you for felony burglary. How old are you? You look like you're about fourteen."

"I'm eighteen!" he said indignantly.

"So, you're an adult?"

"Hey, wait a minute," the kid said, his brain catching up to what he'd said. He was starting to realize just how much trouble he was in.

"What's your name?" she demanded.

"Aren't you supposed to read me my rights or something?"

"You watch a lot of cop shows?" Erin said. "When I arrest you, I'll tell you your rights. Now, we're just having a conversation. I'm Officer O'Reilly. You've already met my partner Rolf. Now, I'm gonna frisk you. We can do this easy or hard, your choice. But if you've got a wallet, I'm gonna find out who you are whether you talk or not."

"Cal," he said.

"Cal what?"

"Huntington."

"Thanks," Erin said. She could hear sirens approaching, almost on time. Dispatch had been a little slow. If the other car had been closer, they might've been able to snag the Corolla that'd fled the scene. They might still get lucky, but she doubted it. "Cal Huntington, you have a problem," she went on. "See, I know you had a couple buddies who pulled this job with you.

But they saw me coming and took off. They left you here, kiddo. Someone's going to take the fall for this. So your choice is, you can pretend to be a tough guy, in which case you'll go to prison and meet some real tough guys who'll teach you what that means, or you can tell me who your so-called friends are, and you can do a deal."

Erin was a beat cop, not a detective, but she still had a feel for when a perp was about to crack. Cal looked down. "It wasn't about the money," he muttered. "They said to leave the cash."

"What were they after?" Erin asked, startled. That didn't sound like a typical smash-and-grab.

Flashing red and blue lights lit up the store. Car doors slammed and officers raced inside, guns drawn. Cal twisted around in surprise.

"Get back on the ground!" Erin snapped, planting her knee again and forcing him down.

The moment was gone, and both of them knew it. Cal might talk back at the precinct, in interrogation, or he might not, but either way, it wouldn't be Erin asking the questions. She sighed. "Cal Huntington, you're under arrest for burglary. You have the right to remain silent. Anything you say can and will be used against you in a court of law. You have the right to an attorney. If you cannot afford an attorney, one will be assigned to you by the court. Do you understand these rights as they have been stated to you?"

By the time she finished the recitation, another cop was standing over her, grinning. "You're gonna have to throw this one back, O'Reilly," he said. "He's under the size limit."

"Shut up, Brunanski," Erin retorted. "If there was a rule we could only arrest guys as fat as you, we'd never get any assholes off the street."

Brunanski made a face and laid his hand on his substantial belly. "You gotta hit me where it hurts?" he said.

"All right, kiddo," Erin said, hoisting Cal to his feet. "Time to take a ride downtown."

Chapter 2

The other officers laid out a roll of crime-scene tape and started snapping pictures. They wouldn't bother the CSI guys with a standard break-in. While they worked, Erin put her prisoner in the back seat of the squad car, next to Rolf's compartment. Rolf eyed him suspiciously, but Cal gave the dog a wide berth.

Erin should've been happy. She'd gotten a righteous collar, caught a burglar in the act. But the car had gotten away, with whoever and whatever was inside, and she had the feeling she was missing something.

"What'd your buddies want uniforms for?" she asked.

"I don't have to tell you nothing," Cal muttered.

"That's right," Erin said. "We've got all we need. You've been caught in the act of burglary in the third degree. You're looking at twenty-seven months, and that's assuming no prior criminal history." While she was talking, she was punching keys on her squad car's computer. "Look what we've got here! Calvin Huntington, age eighteen, vandalism, petty larceny, theft of services, criminal mischief. You've finally made it to the big time, kiddo. This is your first felony. Congratulations. With all those priors, I'd say you're facing, oh, eighty-four months. But if you plead down, give up your partners, who knows? The DA might knock it back to misdemeanor larceny; get you out in under a year. What do you think?"

Cal didn't answer, and Erin didn't really expect him to. He'd retreated inside himself, shutting out the experience. She might as well be talking to one of the store mannequins.

A car pulled up in front of the store. A short, balding man jumped out and hurried toward the building. He was dressed sloppily, in a T-shirt and sweat pants, and had all the look of someone who'd woken up at the wrong time of night. Erin pegged him as the owner of the store.

She left Cal to stew in the back of the car, with Rolf keeping an eye on him, and stepped back onto the sidewalk. As responding officer, it was her job to take a statement from the owner.

The man stopped in front of his damaged establishment and ran his hands through his hair, leaving strands sticking out at odd angles. "Oh no," he said, and apparently liked the sound of it. "Oh no, oh no, oh no."

Erin approached him and put on her official manners. "Sir? I'm Officer O'Reilly. Are you the proprietor of this place of business?"

"Oh, no," he said again. "I mean, yes. Yes, I am."

"What is your name, sir?"

"Bernie... Bernard Feldman."

She went through the usual questions. None of it was interesting, but it had to be done in order to get to the important stuff. There were a few things Erin was very curious about.

"Are you acquainted with a Cal or Calvin Huntington?" she finally asked.

"Calvin? Yes, of course," Bernie said. "He used to work for me."

Bingo. "When was this?" she asked.

"Just last week."

"Why did his employment terminate?"

"I fired him." Bernie blinked nervously. "Should I have said that? Is he in some kind of trouble?"

You have no idea, Erin thought. Out loud, she said, "Why did you fire him?"

"A couple of guys were hanging around the store," Bernie explained. "Calvin said they were friends of his. I told him he couldn't have friends loitering. He got nervous and, uh, defensive. He talked back to me. Then the big one, the one with the tattoo, told me to mind my own business. I told him he was standing in my business, and to get out and never come back. For a second, I thought he was going to, uh, hit me. Then he flicked a finger at my face and stomped out. I told Calvin that if he attracted that kind of person to my store, I didn't want to see him again, either. He said I'd be sorry I said that."

Erin nodded, trying to conceal her growing excitement. "Did you know either of the two guys?"

Bernie shook his head. "I'm sorry, officer. They looked like common street thugs. You know... with the tank-top shirts, the low-hanging pants, the big shoes... wait! The little one, he called the big one something. Jake? That's it: Jake."

"You mentioned a tattoo," Erin said. "Could you describe it?"

"It was a snake, twisted around his arm... the right arm, just under the shoulder. A red and black snake, with yellow eyes."

Erin jotted down the description. "You said he was big. How tall, would you say?"

"Six-two, maybe six-three. He was beefy, too, like he worked out a lot. Big muscles, tight shirt."

"What color was his hair?"

"He didn't have any. His scalp was shaved and he had, um, one of those bandannas."

"I just have a few more questions," Erin said. "Let's go inside. I need you to tell me what's been damaged or stolen."

The police turned on the lights, the bright fluorescents giving a cold, hard light. Bernie stepped gingerly around the broken glass, wringing his hands. He noted that the money was still in the till. Erin had interrupted Cal before he could finish jimmying the register. Several heaps of uniforms were scattered on the floor, like discarded laundry in a teenager's bedroom. "There doesn't seem to be anything missing," he said distractedly. "But I can't be sure until everything is tidied up. Oh dear, oh dear. What a terrible mess."

Erin took a guess. "Mr. Feldman, when the two men, Jake and his friend, were in your store, where were they standing?"

"By that rack over there," he said, pointing.

"What uniforms are these?" she asked, walking over to take a closer look.

"Oh, nothing special," he said. "Those are security-guard uniforms."

Erin's lip curled. Rent-a-cop outfits. Squint a little, and if the light wasn't too good, you might mistake the wearer for a police officer. This rack had been especially harshly handled, shirts and slacks heaped haphazardly. But Erin noticed that only the large and extra-large sizes seemed to have been rifled.

"Mr. Feldman, could you check whether any of these uniforms are missing?" she asked.

"I'd have to look at the inventory," he said. "Do you need an answer right now?"

Erin gave him a card with the precinct's phone number. "It's not urgent," she said. "But if you could give a call to this number when you know, it'd be a big help. Now, we do have a suspect in custody, and I'd like you to identify him."

The rest was routine police work. Bernie knew Cal, just as he'd said, and confirmed the ID. Then, finally, she got back behind the wheel of her car, made sure Rolf was secure, and drove to the precinct to book the prisoner. All the way back, she couldn't shake the question: What did a couple of small-time hoods want with rent-a-cop uniforms?

*   *   *

At the end of a shift, especially the "dog watch" that ran from midnight to eight, Erin always needed a shower. She preferred not to use the showers at the precinct. It wasn't that she felt uncomfortable there, or vulnerable. She used the shower as a ritual to wash off everything she'd seen and felt at work, and she couldn't do that until she was home.

She closed the door of her apartment, slipped the bolt into place, and took a deep breath, letting it out slowly. It was a studio apartment, sparsely furnished. The sun was up, but like anyone working nights, she'd fitted her windows with heavy curtains. She flipped on the kitchen light. Rolf trotted to his dish and waited, tail wagging. He knew he was off duty, and his mouth slowly opened in an expectant smile.

Erin fed her partner, then headed for the bathroom, unfastening her belt with its heavy burden of pistol, extra ammunition, Taser, flashlight, pepper spray, handcuffs, and radio. She took off her uniform jacket, then the bulky bulletproof vest beneath it. While she finished undressing, she started the shower to warm up the water.

After showering, she wrapped a towel around herself and leaned toward the mirror, wiping away the steam. She saw the face of a thirty-four-year-old woman, heart-shaped, with high cheekbones. Her hair was pure black, a startling contrast to her unusually pale skin. Her eyes were bright blue and hadn't yet acquired the hard cynicism of a police veteran, though she'd been on the force almost eleven years. It was the face of an attractive woman, but a tough one. It took a bold man to approach her uninvited.

Erin turned away from her reflection and left the bathroom. She sat down on the edge of her bed and picked up her phone. She hit the speed dial and listened to it ring twice. Then a woman's voice came on the line.

"Hello?"

"Hi, Mom," Erin said, cocking the phone against her shoulder while she pulled on a loose pair of sleep shorts. "I just got off work. Sorry to call so early."

"Oh, it's no trouble, dear," Mary O'Reilly replied. "We just finished breakfast. Your father's out on the porch with the paper."

"Could you get him?" Erin asked. "There's something I want to run by him."

"Police business?"

Erin heard the hint of concern in her mother's tone. Mary O'Reilly had plenty of practice worrying. Sean, Erin's father, was a twenty-five-year veteran of the NYPD. That meant twenty-five years of her mother watching him go out on patrol, trying not to think that each goodbye might be the last. Then, just a couple of years short of his safe retirement, Erin had followed in his footsteps and put on a shield. Her parents never talked to her about her career choice, but Erin always had the feeling her dad was proud of her, while her mom wished she'd been a doctor, like Sean Junior, or a businessman like her second brother, Michael. Tommy, the youngest, didn't exactly have a career, so Erin didn't count him for comparison.

She knew she was hesitating too long. "Yeah, just something strange I came across on my shift," she said in answer to her mom's question.

Mary put her hand over the receiver and called with a voice strengthened by years spent raising four unruly children. "Come to the phone, dear! Erin's calling!"

It took a few moments for Sean O'Reilly to make his way inside. He'd never been lean, and every year of retirement had added bulk around his midsection. "Morning, kiddo," he said. "Everything all right?"

"I'm fine," Erin said, wishing she didn't have to start every conversation with her dad with those words. "I just wanted to pick your brain before I go to sleep."

"Still working the graveyard detail? Back in my day, that was the rookie shift."

Erin smiled. "Yeah, but there's two other kinds of cops who pull the duty. There's screw-ups like Brunanski who can't get off the Lieutenant's shit list, and there are experienced officers he uses to add some backbone to the roster. Since I'm a K-9, everyone says I'm a natural for the dog watch anyway."

Sean chuckled. "Brunanski hasn't been pensioned off? I thought he'd put in his time years ago."

"He's still around, still causing trouble. Just saw him tonight. Say, Dad, I busted a guy trying to break into the register at a uniform store."

"They stock orange jumpsuits? You could've fitted him right there, save the city some time."

She laughed. "No. But get this. The perp had a couple accomplices who booked it when I rolled up. I think they jacked a couple of rent-a-cop outfits."

Sean thought it over. "Sounds like a prank, or some small-time bullshit. Gang initiation, maybe."

"That's the thing, Dad," Erin said. "I don't think the guy I busted was part of the gang. He was just their way into the store. He used to work there, and got fired a few days ago. What if he was planning to hook them up with the uniforms, only once he got sacked, he didn't have access anymore? Then they had to break in."

"Could be," he replied. "You know who the other perps are?"

"Not yet. I'm hoping the kid we've got cuts a deal, gives up the others to save himself a few months. I've got a first name, a description, and a tattoo. And a silver Corolla."

"Probably stolen," her father said. Erin might not see cynical cop-eyes in her mirror, but her dad sure did.

"Probably," she agreed. "But I got the plates, just in case. What do you think I should do?"

"Do?" Sean sounded surprised. "You're a beat cop, kiddo, just like I was. We don't do anything in cases like this. This is one for the detectives, if they bother with it. Which they most likely won't. Theft of uniforms? They're worth what, a couple hundred bucks, tops? Hardly the heist of the century."

"But what if they're planning a bigger job?" Erin asked. "The uniforms might be disguises. How can I stop it?"

"You can try to find out who they are and bust them for the burglary," he said doubtfully. "Then see if you can flip one of them. Otherwise? You wait and see what you read in the papers."

She sighed. "I thought you'd say that."

"Kiddo, we don't usually get to stop the crimes before they happen," he said. "We're only human, and we don't get to bust 'em for what they might do. Anything else on your mind?"

"Nope," Erin said. "I'm gonna catch some Zs. Good night... good morning. Whatever."

"Be careful, kiddo."

"I will. Love you, Dad."

She clicked off her phone, hung up her towel, and pulled on a baggy T-shirt. Then she crawled under the covers and switched off the light. Rolf clambered up beside her and settled himself into a remarkably small, furry ball. Erin laid a hand on her partner's back, closed her eyes, and let go of the night's work.

Chapter 3

Erin had plenty to keep her busy over the course of the following week. The dog watch was never boring. From midnight to eight, most normal people were at home and in bed, but normal people weren't a cop's main concern. Between drug addicts, petty crooks, firebugs, drunk drivers, and general crazies, there were plenty of incidents to fill her reports at the end of each shift. She made four arrests, assisted at six accident scenes, and dealt with the usual patrol work. The most common calls were domestic disturbances, noise complaints, and reports of disorderly conduct. She just about forgot the burglary at the uniform store.

Friday morning, she was summoned into her commander's office. Erin and Rolf were a little frazzled. They'd been the first on scene at an apartment fire. It had been messy and unpleasant, but at least no one had been seriously hurt. Rolf had made a sweep of the ground floor, and in the process both patrolwoman and dog had ended up exhausted, soot-stained, and smelling of smoke. They'd come straight back to the precinct from the blaze. They dragged their feet into the office, where Erin made an attempt at standing at attention. Rolf sat beside her, his ears drooping and his tongue hanging out the side of his mouth in a very unofficial manner.

Lieutenant Murphy, on the other side of the desk, was wide awake and smiling. He was a jovial man with a disreputable red beard, a receding hairline, and a slightly-bulging gut from spending too much time in a building where snacks were a little too readily available. He'd been Erin's CO ever since she'd joined Precinct 116's Patrol Division.

"Good morning, O'Reilly," he said. "Long night?"

"Yes, sir," Erin replied. Her shift should've ended an hour and a half earlier.

"I've got good news for you," Murphy said. "Starting Monday, you're back on days."

"You're pulling me off dog watch?" she asked, startled.

"We've got a couple pieces of fresh meat coming in from the Academy, so the duty roster gets shuffled," he explained. "I've had a request to add a K-9 to the nine-to-five. Congratulations, O'Reilly. You can pretend to be an ordinary working stiff. See you Monday, bright and early. That'll be all. Go home, get cleaned up."

"Uh, thanks, sir," she said. She should've been pleased. Getting to work standard hours was something a lot of officers would kill for. But Erin didn't mind the late shift. That was when things *happened*. She hadn't joined the NYPD just to drive around Queens handing out traffic tickets. Her mind whirling with confusion and fatigue, she saluted and left the office.

She went home and spent the next half hour in the bathtub, washing Rolf. He submitted with good grace, only pinning back his ears a little. Then she showered, slept, woke up, sniffed her hair, and showered again. That took care of most of the smell of smoke. By the time her hair was dry, it was early evening.

Erin's dad had told her there was only one thing an Irish cop wanted to do at the end of a week on the job, and she was her father's daughter. She got dressed, brushed her hair, and headed to the bar.

*   *   *

The Priest was one of her regular haunts. It was just off Union Turnpike, an easy walk from her apartment. It was run by Nate O'Connor, a white-haired, heavyset Irishman who claimed to have been thrown out of the clergy for some transgression or other. "But it was the will of the Almighty," Nate often said, "else how would I have found my true calling?" The drinks were good and cheap, the atmosphere nonthreatening.

Erin took a seat at the bar and nodded to Nate, who ambled over.

"Evening, Officer O'Reilly," he said. "What'll you have?"

"Black Velvet," she said.

The former priest took out a champagne flute and filled it halfway. Then he picked up a spoon, held it upside down over the glass, and carefully poured Guinness stout over it. The beer ran down the sides of the flute to form a floating dark layer atop the clear champagne. Nate carefully slid the beer cocktail across the bar.

"That's an unusual drink," the man to Erin's right observed.

She turned to her fellow patron, raising an eyebrow. He was about her age, tall, slender, good-looking in a mild, pleasant way. His wardrobe was a little too J. Crew for Erin's taste, and she prepared to write him off as a generic yuppie.

"If you don't mind my asking, are you in mourning?" he asked.

Erin looked down at herself. She was wearing a dark red halter top and snug-fitting black slacks, hardly the attire of a grieving woman. "Why would you say that?" she asked, humoring him.

"I believe that's a drink that was developed by the English to commemorate the death of Prince Albert," he answered.

"I'm Irish," she shot back. "The death of a stuck-up Englishman might be more of a celebration."

He grinned. It was a nice smile, a genuine one which showed white, straight teeth. "I'm not Irish, but my great-grandfather's great-grandfather fought the British in 1812, so I'll drink to that." He raised his glass. "Nothing as fancy as what you've got there, just straight Guinness for me."

Oh, what the hell, Erin thought. She clinked her glass against his. "Cheers," she said. "So, let's hear it."

"Hear what?"

"Your line."

"My line?"

"Yeah," she said. "I've heard most of them, so take your shot. A lot of guys lead with, 'So, do you come here often?' Some just go straight for the compliments, or offer to buy the next drink. What's your approach?"

He laughed. "I don't script it," he said. "In a world full of pickup artists, I'm drawing with crayons and trying to stay inside the lines."

It was Erin's turn to laugh. "You're telling me you didn't have that line ready?"

"Guilty as charged," he said. "But I'm not trying to sell a used car or get you to buy life insurance. If all I give you is the same canned spam I give every girl in every bar, what's the point? Let's get the bullshit out of the way, okay?"

"Fine by me," Erin said, intrigued in spite of herself.

"Obviously, I think you're attractive. A guy's not going to strike up a conversation with a girl he just met in a bar unless he likes the look of her. I'd like to get to know you, see if we hit it off. But to get you talking to me, I've got to get noticed. That means I have to say something to catch your attention. But then, if I do all the talking, I still won't know you, and all you'll know about me is that I'm that one guy in the bar who wouldn't shut up."

"I see you've given this a lot of thought," Erin said. She took a sip of her drink. "So how do I respond in this scenario?"

"We tell each other something about ourselves," he said. "I'll go first. Luke Devins. I'm an art appraiser." He extended his hand.

"Erin O'Reilly," she answered. "So, you look at paintings; try to figure out what they're worth?"

"That's right."

"I'll bet that opens up some terrible pickup lines," she said. "All sorts of ways to compare a woman to a priceless piece of art, eyes like jewels, a face like Michelangelo painted it, all that crap?"

Luke flashed his brilliant smile again. "Absolutely."

"You ever traffic in stolen goods?"

He blinked and dropped his hand back to his side, his smile vanishing. "Miss O'Reilly," he said, his voice growing suddenly clipped and formal, "I don't deal personally in works of art, however they were obtained. All I do is provide my clients with an accurate estimate of their market value. If I suspect a work is stolen, I inform the police."

Erin's smile was mischievous. "Good," she said. "Because I'm a cop."

He stared at her, looking for some sign of a joke. "Really?"

"Really."

"I'm glad to hear that," Luke said, his own grin returning. "For a second, I thought I was going to end the evening in the trunk of somebody's car. This isn't a sting operation, is it?

Because I was serious. I don't have anything to do with stolen artwork."

Erin shook her head. "Hey, you started the conversation, not me." She took another sip. "What's an art appraiser doing down here? Shouldn't you be hanging around the swanky downtown galleries?"

"There's an exhibit opening at the Queens Museum, over in Flushing Meadows," he explained. "Have you seen the posters for it? The Orphans of Europe?"

Erin nodded. "I think so. Isn't that the collection of paintings and things they found in Germany?"

"That's right," Luke said. "Some workmen broke through an old tunnel in a salt mine and found a collection of art treasures that had been looted by the Nazis. There were some well-known pieces, but others, no one was sure where they'd come from. Most of the owners are long dead, of course, in the Holocaust, or air raids, or whatever. My firm wants me to take a look at them before the lot goes on the block."

"It's going to be auctioned?" Erin asked.

"Once the tour's done," Luke said. "No one can agree who owns most of it, so Sotheby's in London will auction off the whole collection of unclaimed works, with the proceeds going to the relief of war refugees around the world. The show starts next weekend."

"Does this sort of talk get you laid much?" Erin teased.

Luke laughed and shook his head. "War refugees and art shows aren't really the sort of things that get your average girl hot. I'm talking your ear off, probably boring you to tears. And you still haven't told me much of anything about you."

"That's true," she said. "So why don't you buy me a drink?"

"And then you'll do some talking?"

She met his eye and liked what she saw there. "Sure," she agreed.

*   *   *

"Why become a police officer?" Luke asked.

Erin had lost track of how many rounds of drinks they'd had, but not because she was bingeing. She was too busy talking and listening. Every now and then she took a sip, and when her glass was empty either she or Luke signaled Nate and a full one appeared. She took another swallow and swished the dregs in the bottom of the flute, watching the dark and clear liquids swirl together.

"It wasn't just because of Dad being a cop," she said. "And it wasn't that I wanted to help people. Hell, my brother does that. Sean Junior, I mean. He's a trauma surgeon. He sees more blood and does more good in a day than I do in a week. I guess it's that I see the world in black and white. There's a line, on the one side you've got the civvies, the ordinary Joes who are basically okay, and on the other side are the perps, the bad guys. The blue line between them, that's the cops. That's me. That's what I always wanted."

Luke was matching Erin drink for drink, and the neatly-dressed art appraiser was starting to look a little glassy-eyed. "I get it," he said. "But isn't it a little... well, dangerous?"

"It's not as bad as you think," she said. "Sure, every now and then you get a tough guy, had a few beers, thinks he can take on the whole NYPD. And it doesn't help that I'm small, and a woman. Chivalry is bullshit. There's plenty of guys who will hit a girl. What do you think they do to their wives and girlfriends? But Rolf's a great partner. Your average asshole may want to fight half a dozen cops, but when the paws hit the ground, man, it's all over. How many drunks you think want to tangle with ninety pounds of German Shepherd?"

Luke chuckled. "There's something about the teeth, isn't there?"

Erin smiled. "You want to meet him?"

"Sure," he said. "Like... now?"

"You ought to know something, though," she said. "If you come back to my place tonight, it just means you get to see where I live and meet my dog. I don't go to bed on the first date. If that bugs you, there's plenty of girls you can try your luck with."

"Believe it or not, Erin, not every guy's looking to dive into a woman's pants the first chance they get." He grinned. "Not that the idea didn't occur to me. They *are* very nice pants."

She laughed. "Careful, tough guy. I've got a gun, a Taser, and a trained police dog."

He held up his hands. "No funny business, I promise."

"Okay, then, just so we're clear." She stood up and laid down some cash to cover her part of the bar tab. "You coming?"

Luke paid his bill, drained his last Guinness, and put the empty glass on the counter. Then he followed her out.

*   *   *

Rolf had self-control to spare. Dogs with poor impulse control didn't make it far in K-9 training. When he saw Luke, he did his usual thing when meeting Erin's friends. He gave the man a long, measuring look, then stalked toward him, ears pinned ever so slightly back, tail making a slow sweep. He sniffed disdainfully at the hand Luke cautiously offered, then glanced at Erin, seeking her cue. Seeing that this guy was on good terms with her, he accepted a little scratching behind the ears. Let the Labradors and Golden Retrievers of the world whore themselves out for human attention; Rolf had his professional pride. He circled the newcomer and, without taking his eyes from the man, returned to Erin's side and sat bolt upright, waiting and watching.

"I see what you mean," Luke said. "I would not want to mess with him."

Erin rubbed Rolf's head. "He's friendly enough. He's just not demonstrative. And he takes some time to warm up to new people. If you want to give him a chance, he needs another walk. You want to come along? My head could use some clearing. How many Black Velvets did I have?"

"I wasn't counting," he said. "How much Guinness did I knock back?"

She shrugged. "Beats me." She clipped Rolf's leash to his collar. Then, to Luke's surprise, she fastened her holstered Glock to her belt at the small of her back.

"You really need that?" he asked.

"It's not a bad neighborhood," she said, "but after ten you want to be careful. The dog keeps muggers away, but I'd feel pretty silly if I needed my piece and didn't have it."

"Why didn't you bring it to the bar?"

She smiled with false innocence. "I used to. But it seems to scare the men away. Do you have a gun?"

"Good Lord, no," Luke laughed. "I'm a... what did you call it? A civvie?"

"I'll just have to protect you, then," she said.

They walked together, the night air cool and refreshing. Erin listened to the sounds of the street, her police instincts poised for anything out of place: an angry voice, a squeal of tires, breaking glass. But the streets were quiet tonight. She was very conscious of the man at her side. It had been a while since she'd been out with a guy. Working nights played hell with her social life. She remembered what her father had said to her mother when she started working the dog watch.

"Well, Mary, you can stop worrying about Erin. You said we could put her in a convent, but I said being a cop would work out the same."

"What's so funny?" Luke asked.

"Oh, nothing," Erin said. "Just remembering something."

Luke looked down at his wrist. "Oh, damn," he said. "I didn't realize it was this late. I... Erin, I really don't want to say this, but I've got a morning meeting. Eight o'clock. I should've been heading back an hour ago. I knew I should've got a hotel in Queens. The commute from downtown is a killer."

They had stopped under a corner streetlight. Erin looked at his face. He seemed genuinely unhappy to be leaving. "If you've got to go, you've got to go," she said. "I'm hardly in a position to bitch about other peoples' schedules. You okay to drive?"

"I took a cab down," he said. "I've got a car, but I don't take it out much. You know New York traffic."

"And New York parking," she agreed.

"Listen, Erin," he said, "I'm very glad I met you tonight. This is cliché as hell, but I'd like to see you again. Here's my number." He handed her a business card that appeared like a magician's sleight-of-hand.

"You want mine?" she replied.

"Nine-one-one?" he guessed.

She shook her head, smiling. "You're not what I expected."

"Neither are you. Yes, I'd like your number."

She gave it to him. "I'm working days starting next week. So I'll be available after about six."

"There's an evening gala a week from today," he said. "The Orphans exhibit I told you about. I don't know if you like European art, or if you were just pretending to be interested, but..."

"Sure," Erin said quickly, without thinking. "That sounds nice. You can tell me what it's all worth."

"I'll do that," he said. He started to turn away, paused, and turned back to face her. He stepped forward and bent toward her.

Erin flinched. Luke never realized just how close he came to catching a reflexive palm-strike under the chin. But he wasn't moving aggressively. He kissed her lightly on the lips.

"Goodnight, Erin," he said.

"Goodnight, Luke," she replied, still confused. Then he was gone. She raised a hand to her face and smiled to herself. Then she looked down at Rolf, who stared back with an expression of mild curiosity.

"What are you looking at?" she demanded.

He slowly opened his jaws and let his tongue roll out in an unmistakable smile.

"Shut up, furball," she said. "Come on, it's time we got to bed."

Chapter 4

The week before the gala was busy, but unmemorable. Erin had switched over from nights to day shifts before, but it always took some getting used to. Monday and Tuesday, her head felt like it was stuffed full of cotton balls. She kept waking up in the middle of the night. The daylight glare made her head hurt, so she wore sunglasses most of the time. That was okay, since every police officer was more intimidating behind a pair of reflective shades. She made a mental note to see if some novelty store made dark glasses for dogs.

All the time, whether writing out a ticket, responding to a domestic disturbance, or asking an old woman what exactly she meant by "suspicious activity" in her next-door neighbor's backyard, she kept thinking about Luke. She felt silly, but she couldn't help it. She *liked* him. He was funny, charming, intelligent, and handsome. And he liked her, too. It had been a long time between boyfriends, and maybe, she told herself, she was feeling a little overloaded by positive male attention. Whatever would her dad say?

Nonetheless, when Luke called Thursday night, she practically pounced on the phone. Then she took a deep breath, composed herself, and said "Hello?" in her most nonchalant tone.

"Erin? This is Luke... Luke Devins," he said, sounding much more nervous on the phone than he had been in person.

"Hey, Luke," she said. "How's it going?"

"I'm all right... Say, the grand opening at the museum will be tomorrow. You might have made other plans, but..."

"No!" Erin interrupted, then silently cursed herself for being too eager. "I mean, I was planning on it. If you'd still like me to come, that is." Damn, what was the matter with her? Now she was simpering like some ditzy teenager on prom night. "Your other date ditch you or something?"

"No!" Luke exclaimed. He paused. "I can pick you up at seven, or you can meet me there if you'd prefer, but parking's going to be tight. I'm there by invitation, so I've got a spot reserved. The gates officially open at eight."

"Ooh, a man with his own parking space," she said. "Is that supposed to make me swoon?"

"No, but it'll probably go easier on your high heels than walking half a mile," he said. "It's formal, by the way."

"So I should show up in my dress blues?" Without waiting for his answer, she added, "You'll be wearing a tux?"

"Of course," he replied.

"Well, that's something to look forward to, at least," she said. "See you at seven." Then she hung up, on the principle that it was better to leave men wanting more.

*   *   *

Erin didn't really own much formal clothing. Her options for this sort of event were limited to the "little black dress" she'd had over a decade, and was proud she could still fit into; a dark red number with a neckline that was a little too daring for a first real date; and a full-length, midnight-blue dress with a slit partway up the side that was slinky and form-fitting without promising too much. Or she could've gone with what she'd said to Luke and worn her dress uniform. She went with the blue gown instead.

Her hair presented a problem. She could never quite bear the thought of cutting it all off, and at work she settled for a sensible ponytail, but that wouldn't do for a formal occasion. Besides, who wanted to waste an hour being dolled up by a stylist who didn't know how to shut up? She settled on a bun, but since she was doing it herself, in front of her bathroom mirror, a few strands wandered free. A single lock of hair hung down in front of her right cheek in an attractive way, but that was mostly accidental. She kept her makeup minimal, just lipstick and mascara.

That left jewelry to figure out, and she didn't have many options. A small pair of pearl studs, an academy graduation gift from her mother, went in her ears. She had to rummage through her dresser to find the old pearl necklace she'd inherited from her grandmother to complete the ensemble.

Erin glanced at the clock. Even though she'd opted for a very simple look, compared to what a lot of the women there would be wearing, she'd used up all her prep time. She just had time to feed Rolf before Luke's car pulled up in front of the apartment.

She felt ridiculous as she walked down the apartment steps. Here she was, dressed totally impractically, without her dog, her shield, or her gun. She didn't need to be playing dress-up with this guy she barely knew. She ought to call the whole thing off. It had been a long week, her sleep schedule was still out of whack, and—

Hmm. Luke really did look good in a tuxedo. He was opening the car door for her and even bowing a little. There was a smile on his face as he looked at her, and it wasn't because he was noticing how poor a job she'd done on her hair. He was admiring her, enjoying looking at her, and it didn't give her the creeps the way it sometimes did in the precinct break room. Maybe this wasn't such a bad idea after all.

"Good evening," he said. "You're looking very nice tonight."

"You clean up okay," she said, sliding onto the car seat. "Let's get this show on the road."

*   *   *

Erin hadn't been to the Queens Museum of Art since she was a little girl. She remembered being fascinated by the museum's permanent centerpiece, a massive panorama of New York City with every building lovingly rendered. She'd eagerly searched for her own house, to the amusement of her brothers and parents, and been amazed at the sheer size of the city, hundreds of thousands of tiny apartments, skyscrapers, churches, parks, and office buildings. Now, riding down Grand Central Parkway in Luke's silver Lexus, she felt a little bit of that girlish thrill again.

He was spouting trivia about the museum, something about it having been built for the 1939 World's Fair, but Erin wasn't really interested in the facts. She craned her neck as the building came into view.

Her heart sank. The museum's façade was marred by cranes and scaffolding. Jersey barriers channeled cars past the ceremonial entrance. Big construction dumpsters stood at the foot of the walls.

"The renovation project will be finished in October, or maybe November," Luke explained. "Some of the galleries are closed."

"Strange time for a gala," Erin said.

"It's when the show was available," he said. "Once you get inside, it's really very nice. They're almost done with the construction work. The exterior is all that's left. They hope this exhibit will draw attention to the new building."

"Doesn't the remodeling make for a security risk?" the cop in Erin made her ask.

Luke laughed. "There's going to be dozens of guards there," he said. "They've brought in extras for the event."

"Rent-a-cops," she scoffed.

"Maybe, but they've still got guns," he said.

"And I don't," Erin said.

"Does that bother you?"

"A little," she confessed. "But I can hardly bring one into a formal party. Where would I carry it? All I've got is this tiny little handbag, and it barely fits my phone. I gotta get a holdout piece, something I can keep hidden. Men are lucky. Their dress clothes have pockets."

He smiled. "I hadn't considered all the concealed-weapon possibilities in a tuxedo."

"What, haven't you ever seen a Bond flick?" she asked, grinning.

Luke might rate preferential parking, but it was still a good walk to the museum, especially since they had to go around to the far side. They passed the Unisphere, a gigantic stainless-steel globe that towered twelve stories above Flushing Meadows. They paused to take in the huge sculpture, which seemed to float on a cushion of water-jets from the fountains around it. Other couples in tuxes and evening gowns were doing the same, enjoying the slanting evening sunlight and the fresh air.

They made their way into the museum, Luke flashing his special badge to the guards at the door. Erin was pleased to see that, rent-a-cops or not, the men at the entrance were taking their responsibilities seriously. They checked every ID. Even though she was accompanying one of the event's privileged guests, they still scanned her driver's license and glanced at her face. She instinctively noted the guns at their belts, Sig-Sauer automatics. Those were good, reliable guns. Several officers at her own precinct carried sidearms just like them.

Inside, they found a sunken courtyard with a ceiling made entirely of glass, held up by a framework of steel girders. There were tables with refreshments to one side, a crowd of VIPs mingling, and a string quartet playing something dreary that Erin didn't care for. Then again, while she was an excellent shot, a keen judge of character, and a skilled law-enforcement officer, she couldn't carry a tune to save her life.

Two men approached Luke. One was heavyset—no, Erin decided, he was *fat*. Everything about him was round, from his bald head to his belly to the tips of his shiny black shoes. He had a big, round laugh and a broad smile planted on his round face. He looked like exactly the sort of man she expected to see at this sort of event. His companion, on the other hand, gave her pause. His face had too many lines in it. She thought, suddenly and incongruously, of the guys who stood beside freeway entrance ramps with cardboard signs in their hands. This man looked like a homeless bum dressed up in a tux as some sort of joke. His face was weathered and lined, his eyes hard and quick.

"Luke, my boy!" exclaimed the fat man, seizing Luke's hand and pumping it enthusiastically. His accent was that of a well-educated Englishman. "So glad you could join us!" He thumped the younger man's shoulder with his free hand.

"Good to see you again, Van," Luke said, staggering a little under the onslaught. "Erin, this is Dr. Phineas Van Ormond. He lectures at Cambridge on Renaissance art. Dr. Van Ormond, this is Erin O'Reilly."

"Miss O'Reilly!" the professor said with evident delight. He took her hand and bowed, planting a kiss on it to Erin's consternation. "Please, all my friends and colleagues call me Van. I hope to count you among the former, if perhaps not the latter. And what do you do in the world of art?"

"I did some watercolors in third grade," she said. "Mom put one on the fridge. My teacher said I had potential." Now that she was standing closer to him, she could see that his suit, though expensive, was looking a little worn around the edges. Maybe he wasn't as rich as she'd thought.

Van Ormond blinked, momentarily at a loss. Then he gave another of his room-filling laughs. "Marvelous!" he exclaimed. "Charming, utterly charming."

"I spent a semester at college studying abroad," Luke explained to Erin. "I attended Van's classes on the Italian masters."

"One of my very finest students," Van Ormond said, clapping Luke on the shoulder again. "I always knew he would do great things. He—"

The other man, the gaunt, weathered one, stepped suddenly past Van Ormond to regard Luke with his hard, intense stare. The portly professor fell abruptly silent, though the other man hadn't said anything, hadn't even looked at him.

"*Herr* Devins," the skinny man said, his German accent unmistakable. "Have you seen her?"

"I beg your pardon," Luke said, raising an eyebrow. "I don't think we've met, sir?"

"Rudolf Schenk," the man said. "Humboldt Universität, Berlin."

"*Herr* Professor," Luke said with sudden respect. "I have read many of your articles with great interest." He offered his hand.

Schenk ignored it. "Have you seen her?" he repeated.

"Seen who?" Erin asked blankly, casting a glance around at the crowd. Her brain, corrupted by pop culture, was already trying to identify whatever actress or tabloid icon this strange man might mean.

"The Madonna," Luke said, understanding.

"Madonna's here?" Erin asked, not understanding at all.

Luke laughed. "Not that Madonna, Erin. *The* Madonna. That's what she's being called. The Madonna of the Water. She's a painting. Probably an unknown Raphael. I've only seen her in photos, but—"

"There is no 'probably', *Herr* Devins," Schenk interrupted. "She *is* a Raphael, an original."

"Think of it!" effused Van Ormond. "An undiscovered work by one of the true masters! In near-pristine condition! What value could be put on such a find? At auction, if it proves genuine... why, millions at the least!"

"If she's authentic," Luke said, "she's priceless. But I'll need to get a closer look. Erin, do you want to see what all the fuss is about?"

Erin nodded. "I'm game. After all, we're here to see the art, right?"

"Wrong," Schenk said. He stared straight into Erin's eyes, and it took everything she had not to flinch away. She didn't feel that she was looking at a stodgy old professor. And she wasn't thinking of a homeless bum now. He reminded her of the little kids she'd seen in bad neighborhoods, kids whose parents were junkies and deadbeats. Schenk wasn't a young man, he was fifty at least, but his eyes were far, far older than the rest of him. He looked like a man who'd taken a guest tour of Hell. "Art is not merely to be seen, *Fräulein* O'Reilly," he continued. "Art is a part of us, of our experience. Its history is added to the artist's original inspiration. Every hand which holds it, every palace and chamber it adorns, every sale, every theft, every murder done for the sake of it... Art is humanity. And like humanity, its history is written in crime and blood. Do you understand?"

"I think I do," Erin replied with a wry smile. "I'm a cop."

Chapter 5

Most art galleries were sparse, white spaces, with paintings isolated from one another by large patches of blank wall. For the Orphans of Europe, the museum had done something very different. The gallery was black. Black velvet curtains hung at intervals along its length, dividing the space into small rooms. Each room was furnished in the style of the 1940s with old radio sets, armchairs and coffee tables. The effect was somber and a little eerie. Some clever decorator had put little homey touches into the furnishings. Erin saw a pipe just like the one her grandfather used to smoke after dinner, sitting unattended beside an ashtray. Her stomach twisted and she looked away.

The paintings hung amid the everyday things of that long-gone era. The visitors passed portraits, landscapes, still lives, abstract combinations of geometric shapes. These were pieces which had indeed been orphaned, torn from their owners and hidden from the world for decades.

"It's like a time capsule," Erin said in a low voice.

Even the gregarious Van Ormond spoke in a near-whisper. "Yes, my dear," he said. "Just imagine being one of the finders, going into the salt mine and finding so many treasures!"

"And no one knows what happened to the owners?" she asked.

"Disappeared," Schenk growled. "They went up the chimneys, in the camps."

"In the Holocaust?" Erin had learned a little about World War II in school, but history had never been her strongest subject.

The grim professor nodded. "*Ja, Fräulein.*"

"We don't know that for certain," Van Ormond objected. "The Nazis robbed practically everybody. When Hermann Göring's treasure was recovered from Neuschwanstein, the Yanks found items looted from museums and private collections all over Europe. Many of the owners were located, still alive. The public artifacts were returned to the proper museums."

Erin nodded. Luke was listening with polite interest, but he had eyes only for the paintings. His face was thoughtful and intent. He often stooped close, cocking his head to take in each picture from multiple angles.

"So, do you see one you like?" she teased.

"The Madonna is in the next room," Luke said. "Come on."

They ducked past the curtain and found themselves alone with the Madonna of the Water.

Erin had never really understood the attraction of fine art. She was impressed by the amount of skill it had taken, of course, and the thought that she was staring at something another person had made a hundred or a thousand years ago was kind of cool, but mostly it left her unmoved. But here she came face to face with a true masterpiece.

The Madonna was small, the whole painting only about two feet on a side. She appeared to be a young woman, but with a serenity that made her age hard to guess. Her eyes were mostly closed, staring thoughtfully at something just over Erin's shoulder. Her lips turned up in just a hint of a smile, reminding

Erin of the famous expression on the Mona Lisa's face. In the background was a gently rolling seascape. The colors were as rich and bright as if they had just been painted.

Erin caught herself reaching toward the painting. She felt a strange longing to step into it, to curl into the arms of that motherly figure. Her own mother was a stout, redheaded Irishwoman, nothing at all like this placid and holy portrait, but Erin didn't care.

"Lovely, isn't she?" Luke murmured.

"Wow," Erin breathed.

"What is your professional opinion, Mr. Devins?" Van Ormond asked, startling them back into themselves.

Luke rubbed his chin and bent toward the picture. A layer of protective glass prevented him from touching or even breathing on the centuries-old painting, but he got as close as he could without coming in contact with the shield. "It's a cabinet painting, certainly the correct age," he said slowly. "The paint is laid on very thickly, with hints of cracking. The composition is consistent with his known works. It's very reminiscent of the Madonna in the Meadow, but here she is by herself instead of with the Christ child." He straightened up. "Gentlemen, this is certainly the work of a great master from the early 1500s, either a Raphael, one of his imitators, or maybe a Perugino."

Erin cleared her throat. "I understood about a third of that," she said. "You said the paint was cracked. Is that bad?"

He shook his head. "No, it's good. It comes from using too much resin in the varnish on the paint, and it's one of the known faults in Raphael's work. It speaks to the authenticity of the piece. If the cracks weren't there, she wouldn't be his."

"I don't believe you guys," Erin said. "You see something like... like *this*, and you look for cracks in the paint. Can't you just... I don't know, look at her?"

"It's my job, Erin," Luke said gently. "Could you look at a mug shot and just see whether it was a good-looking guy?"

She smiled, getting it. "No, I'd be looking for distinguishing marks, tattoos, and the look in his eyes. So, what's a cabinet painting?"

"A painting that was done for a private collector, to be stored in a cabinet for home display," Luke explained. "That's probably why we've never heard of this one."

"Raphael executed a great many cabinet paintings for many patrons," Van Ormond broke in. "He was immensely prolific, though he only lived thirty-seven years. In that respect he was much like Mozart. Such men of genius never seem long for this world."

"What's that?" Erin asked suddenly, pointing to the lower corner of the painting. There were a few speckles of something dark brown.

"Environmental contamination," Luke said. "Being shuffled all over Europe wasn't good for these paintings. Many of them are damaged in some way or another. The handlers can sometimes clean them, but they have to be extremely careful." He grinned at her. "Now who's looking for imperfections?"

"You're doing your job," she said. "I'm doing mine. Those are bloodstains. It's the sort of spatter pattern you get from an exit wound." She glanced at Schenk, who nodded.

"Meaning what, exactly?" Luke said, looking suddenly uncomfortable.

"I'd guess someone was shot, standing right about... here." Erin moved a step back and two steps to her left. "Your Madonna's lucky, Luke. She almost took one right in the face."

"I don't believe this," Luke muttered. "I bring a girl who happens to be a cop to an art exhibit and she starts investigating a murder seventy years old."

Erin shrugged. "Without knowing where the painting was, and who was in the room, I wouldn't be able to build a case. Anyway, it's not a murder investigation if there's no body. Maybe the victim survived."

Van Ormond laughed, but Luke and Professor Schenk didn't.

They lingered in the Madonna's room a while longer. Erin didn't want to leave. She kept looking from the long-dried drops of blood to the placid half-smile on the Madonna's face. At last, she shook herself free of the painting's spell and moved on to see the rest of the exhibit.

Chapter 6

"Well? What do you think?" Luke asked. They were standing near the refreshment table, sipping punch. The two professors had split apart and moved off, Van Ormond to mingle with other guests, Schenk to brood in a corner over a glass of wine.

"Amazing," Erin said.

"I'm sorry about Van and Professor Schenk," he said. "I'd hoped for this to feel more like a date."

Erin smiled at him. "Don't worry, I'm having a good time. I figured it was part of your clever plan. Compared to the two of them, you're practically irresistible. What's with Schenk, anyway?"

"What do you mean?"

"I'm not talking about his manners," she said.

"Or lack of them," he put in. "That's why I was apologizing for him."

"No, I mean, what's his problem? He seems really intense, almost angry."

"He takes all this a little personally," Luke said. "He's older than he looks, Erin. He was born in a refugee camp after the war.

His parents were German Jews. They lived through the Holocaust, but most of their relatives didn't. His father killed himself in 1962."

"Jesus, no wonder he's pissed," Erin said. "Did he tell you that?"

"Nope. Wikipedia," Luke said with a wink. "He's written a lot about reclaimed Nazi treasures. He's one of the main authorities in the field. I've read most of what he's written, and—"

Erin never found out what Luke was about to say. There was a harsh buzz of an alarm. Then an angry shout cut through the murmured conversations.

"Hey! Freeze! You, right there!"

A spike of hot, pure adrenaline shot through Erin. She reflexively dropped a hand to her nonexistent gun belt, then cursed silently as her hand found nothing but the smooth satin of her dress. She stepped forward and threw out an arm, brushing Luke back behind her.

A woman screamed. Several guards started running, two of them drawing their guns. There was a sound of a scuffle. Then four rent-a-cops emerged from the curtained gallery, two of them dragging a struggling fifth man. His hands were zip-tied behind his back. One of the unattached guards was carrying a mailing tube and a black duffel bag. The other had his gun drawn to cover his comrades.

The other security guards formed a half-circle around the five men. "I didn't do anything!" the cuffed man screamed. "Help! Help!"

Erin instinctively moved toward the commotion, even as most of the partygoers drew back in alarm. The guy the guards were holding was dressed in a tuxedo, the same as the other male guests. He looked to be in his mid-thirties, well-groomed.

It was a good disguise for an art thief, she thought. Very James Bond.

The chief guard approached the four. "What's going on?" he snapped.

"He busted the glass and cut the painting out of its frame," the man with the mailing tube explained. "He rolled it up and stuffed it in here, but he wasn't fast enough." He gestured to the prisoner, who continued struggling and protesting. "You're going to jail, asshole."

"Which painting?" the chief demanded.

"Which one do you think?" the one with the tube shot back. "Listen, we better get him out of here. Can you take him somewhere secure, until the cops get here?"

"Okay, sure." The chief guard seemed out of his depth, confused and worried. "We'll hold him at the security station. I'll take custody."

"You better take the painting, too." The man handed over the mailing tube to his superior.

The guests had begun to press back in, muttering and asking questions. The rent-a-cops, heavily outnumbered, were in danger of losing control of the situation. Erin wished again for a gun and a shield. She settled for snatching out her cell phone and punching "1". 911 was short enough for most people, but Erin knew seconds counted in a crisis, and she'd programmed it on speed-dial.

"911 Emergency," Dispatch said crisply, picking up on the first ring. It must be a slow night.

"This is Officer O'Reilly, shield four six four oh," she said. "I've got a ten-thirty-one at the Queens Museum. Single white male, ten-twelve with on-site security." Her code designated a burglary in progress, but that the suspect was in custody.

"Ten-four, O'Reilly," Dispatch replied. "We confirm an alarm triggered at your location. We're sending a cruiser."

"Ten-four," Erin said.

"Erin, what is going on?" Luke demanded.

"Art heist," she said. "Some jackass thought he could swipe a painting. Now he's learning the error of his ways."

She watched as the man in the tux, continuing to protest, was marched toward the security station. The other guards were spreading out and splitting up, several of them hurrying to secure the crime scene in the gallery, others moving to cover the exits. Erin approved. They were acting like professionals.

But something wasn't quite right, some little detail nagging at the corner of her mind. She replayed the scene in her head. She tried a trick her dad had taught her. Closing her eyes, she took a slow, deep breath. When she opened them, she'd look at the whole scene with fresh eyes, taking nothing for granted.

Even before she looked, she knew what was happening. It was a shell game. In a good con, the whole point was to keep the marks—not only the guards, but everyone there, including herself—looking at the wrong thing altogether. As a con man would say, the trick wasn't to get the mark to pick the wrong shell. The trick was to get them to pick any shell at all. Of course everyone was looking at the prisoner. Why wouldn't they? The guards were just doing their jobs...

The guards. "Oh, shit," Erin said. She couldn't be sure it was the same men, but four guys in rent-a-cop outfits were at the outside doors. And one of them was still carrying the duffel bag.

Luke had his hand on Erin's bare shoulder, asking her a question, but there was no time to answer. She shrugged away his hand, hit the speed-dial on her phone again, kicked off her high heels, and started to run barefoot across the smooth museum floor.

"911 Emergency," Dispatch said at once, bless them.

"O'Reilly, four six four oh," she said in fast, short bursts. She was halfway to the door, but the men were already outside, they had guns, and she had no idea what she was going to do if she caught them. "There's four thieves at the museum. Dressed as guards. Black duffel bag. Painting inside."

"O'Reilly, repeat," Dispatch came back. "Did you say the thieves were dressed as guards?"

"Yes, dammit!" Erin snapped. She was almost to the doors, but she was too far away.

"Ten-four, O'Reilly," said the imperturbable voice on the other end of the line. Then Dispatch put her on hold.

"Hold it, ma'am!" one of the guards at the door said. "You can't go out there!"

Erin swerved around him. He made a clumsy lunge, missed her, and fell over. Cursing herself for sixteen different kinds of fool, she shoved the door open and raced outside. She hadn't realized how late it had gotten. She and Luke had spent a long while in the gallery. The sun had gone down and the park's lights had come on, illuminating the giant shape of the Unisphere. Beneath it she could see four dark shapes, jogging through the twilight.

Erin kept running. The concrete was rough through the bottoms of her nylons, but she didn't care. She wasn't trying to catch up now, just stay close enough. As long as she could keep the perps in sight, she could direct the cops straight to them. Forcing a confrontation would be pointless and dangerous.

A car was parked at the Avenue of the States. Erin wasn't surprised to recognize it as a silver Corolla. Everything was making sense, a few crucial minutes too late.

Sirens. Oh, thank God, sirens. Blue and red lights flashed as a squad car, tires squealing, pulled up between Erin and her quarry. Its driver's-side door swung open and a cop tumbled out, pistol in hand.

"Freeze, police!" he shouted, leveling his gun at the men.

Erin recognized Officer Brunanski by his voice. That figured. All the cops in Queens, and he'd have to be the closest. At least it was someone she knew. She angled toward the squad car and opened her mouth to yell.

Three muzzle flashes flared in the near-dark. The flat, sharp cracks of gunshots echoed across the park. A bullet hole appeared in the squad car's window. Brunanski gave a grunt, as if he'd been punched in the stomach, and sat down hard.

Erin dropped into a crouch behind the engine block of the car. "Brunanski!" she called. "It's O'Reilly. You okay?"

"I dunno," he answered in a breathless whisper. "Bastards... shot me."

Erin dropped her phone to the pavement, yanked open the passenger-side door, and leaned in, keeping her body as low as possible. She snatched up the dangling radio receiver. "O'Reilly here," she gasped. "Ten-thirteen, forthwith. All available units. Shots fired, officer down. Repeat, officer down!"

There was the briefest of pauses. Then Dispatch was on the line again. The calm, impersonal voice now carried a very hard edge. "All available units are inbound to your location. Paramedics en route."

Erin wormed her way across the seat of the squad car to the driver's side. Another couple of gunshots rang out, but they didn't even hit the car. Brunanski was sitting against the back door of the car, one hand clamped across his substantial gut. He was still holding his pistol in his other hand. When he saw Erin, he reversed the grip on the gun and held it out to her. She took it from him and wriggled out onto the pavement, dropping into a crouch and taking aim. Brunanski was an old-school cop, with a grandfathered sidearm. Instead of the Glock automatic Erin carried, his service weapon was a .38 Police Special revolver. It felt a little odd in Erin's hand, but she'd practiced with the same type of weapon and was confident she could use it. Right now she wanted nothing more than to blow the bastards right out of their shoes. But her first duty was to a fellow officer. Keeping the gun directed toward the perps, she asked, "Where you hit?"

"Low down," the officer groaned. "Right under the vest."

Shit, Erin thought. Abdominal wounds were some of the worst. She risked a quick glance at him. Police body armor had decent coverage down to the stomach, but Brunanski was overweight and his vest rode a little too high on his bulky body. It had been a terribly lucky shot from the escaping thieves, narrowly missing the door panel of the squad car and skimming under the Kevlar of Brunanski's vest. A lot of blood was seeping through the policeman's fingers.

"Okay, keep pressure on it," she said to him, eyes scanning the shadows. She didn't have a target. At least they weren't taking fire anymore. She brought her gaze back to the silver Corolla at the sound of its engine coming to life. "Stay still."

She didn't wait for an answer. She was already on her feet, both hands clasped on the revolver's grip. The range was long for pistol shooting, about fifty yards, and in the dark she'd have to get lucky. Without knowing what, or who, was behind the target vehicle, departmental rules said she wasn't supposed to fire. Erin didn't care. She didn't see any bystanders in her line of fire, and these sons of bitches had just shot a cop.

The Corolla's tires squealed. The little car accelerated, heading north. Erin took two steps forward, cleared the squad car's door, drew in a breath, and squeezed the trigger six times in rapid succession. At least one bullet hit home. The car's rear driver's-side window shattered. Pebbles of broken safety glass sparkled under the streetlights. Then the car was out of range, picking up speed, and the revolver was empty.

She turned back to the radio, dropping the smoking gun onto the driver's seat. "Suspect vehicle northbound on Avenue of the States. Silver Corolla, left rear window broken. Four suspects, armed and dangerous." That duty done, she returned her attention to the downed officer.

"It's okay, Brunanski," she said. "I've got you. Help's on the way." She went for the first-aid kit in the squad car and opened the little metal case, keeping up her reassuring chatter. "Talk to me, man. Can you move your legs?"

"I... I don't... know," he muttered. "Cold."

She ripped open a packet of QuickClot hemostat. "This is gonna hurt, buddy, but I have to stop the bleeding. Keep talking." She unbuttoned the bottom couple of buttons of his uniform shirt so she could see the wound. There was so much blood, it was tricky to find. She located the surprisingly small hole by feel. He gasped in pain at the touch. She clamped the mesh bag of clotting agent onto the injury. "Can you keep pressure here?"

"Hands... shaky," he said, his voice slurring with the onset of shock.

"Okay, that's fine," she said, trying to keep the tremor out of her own voice. "I've got it." She had her own hand over the wound, pressing tight. "Keep talking, Brunanski, you ugly Polack. You stay with me." She was feeling a little shocky herself. Where was the goddamn ambulance? Where was the backup?

Even in the dim light of the park, she could see that Brunanski was deathly white. He'd probably taken one in the liver. Maybe, if the ambulance showed up fast, and if they got him to an emergency room in the next few minutes, he might live. There was nothing more she could do for a gut wound.

Sirens filled the air, coming rapidly nearer. She heard running feet behind her. Half a dozen museum security—real museum security—hurried up. The security chief bent over her.

"What can I do?" he asked.

"There should be a blanket in the trunk," she said. "He's in shock. We've got to keep him warm."

The man fumbled with the trunk release, got it open, and came back with a military blanket. They wrapped it around the downed officer as best they could, while Erin kept pressure on the wound.

"Damn it, don't you know your own people?" she demanded through gritted teeth. "Couldn't you see those guys weren't yours?"

The security chief shrugged helplessly. "They brought in, like, a dozen new guys for the gala," he said. "I'd never seen half of them before tonight."

"Jesus," she swore. "I hope your employer's real goddamn happy."

"O'Reilly...?" Brunanski murmured. "Erin?"

"Yeah, John, I'm here," she said, feeling funny at the sudden use of first names. She took his hand in hers, keeping her other hand tight against his stomach. The blood just wasn't stopping.

"I was... careless. Sorry."

"You were doing your job," she said. "They just got lucky. We'll get them. I'll get them. I promise."

"Tired," he whispered. His eyes were closed. His hand squeezed hers for a moment, then went limp.

The ambulance howled down the avenue, lights flashing. Almost before the wheels stopped turning, the paramedics were out and running to the downed officer. Erin allowed the security men to steer her away from the scene, letting the EMTs take over the first aid.

Someone draped a tuxedo coat over her bare shoulders. Erin clutched at it gratefully, leaving smears of blood on the lapel. She was shivering, mostly from emotion. Luke was there, putting an arm around her.

"Are you okay?" he asked.

She nodded numbly.

"I've... got your shoes," he said, holding them up by the ankle straps.

"Thanks," she said absently. Luke led her to a nearby park bench. She sank down on it, her whole body trembling with tension. To her embarrassment, she realized there were tears in her eyes.

Chapter 7

Luke offered to drive her home, but Erin flatly refused. Her moment of weakness was past, replaced by an anger which astonished her with its force. She couldn't possibly sit on the sidelines. She had to give her report to the other officers on scene. There was evidence to collect, witnesses to interview, work to do.

"You should give a statement, then go home," she said to Luke. "I'm going to be up all night."

"I think you'd do better to get some rest," he countered. "Problems are always easier to solve after a good night's sleep."

"You think I can sleep after this?" she demanded. "I know what needs solving. I can do it just fine."

"That's not what I meant," he said, holding up a hand. "I just think—"

"Do you know where they're taking the Madonna?" she demanded. "You know art dealers. Where would they go to sell her?"

"I don't know," he said.

"Then get out of the way and let me find it!" she snapped. "Let me do my damn job!"

She saw the hurt in his face, but she couldn't take it back, not then. She handed him his bloodstained coat without another word and turned back to the crime scene. She was wearing a mangled evening gown, her hair hung in a draggled mess around her neck, and her hands and arms were streaked with blood, but in that moment, Erin O'Reilly was every inch a cop.

The museum crawled with police. What would have been a simple theft investigation had graduated to a major operation on account of Brunanski's shooting. A couple of detectives had already arrived on scene, along with a forensic van and half a dozen squad cars. She was pleased to see her own boss, Lieutenant Murphy, talking with a lieutenant from 107th Precinct. She paused only to put her shoes back on, then hurried over to him.

"Sir!" she called.

He looked at her in surprise. "O'Reilly? What are you doing here?" He took in her appearance. "You're not on duty."

"The hell I'm not," she said. "I was here. I saw the whole thing go down." She drew him aside and explained the ruse the thieves had used to slip the painting out of the museum. "I should've known," she finished. "I knew about the security-guard uniforms."

"You did?"

"Yeah. Remember the uniform-store robbery, about two weeks back?"

"Oh, yeah. You think these were the same guys?"

"I think they were gearing up for this job," she said.

"You'd better tell the detectives," Murphy said.

"It'll be in my report," she said. "Where's the kid we took in that night? Cal Huntington?"

He shrugged. "He posted bail. He's out, pending trial. It was a half-assed burglary, and he's basically still a kid. The D.A. wasn't playing hardball."

"I need his address."

Murphy took her by the shoulders, then let go hurriedly, awkward at coming in contact with her bare skin above her dress. "Erin, you're a beat cop, a K-9. This is detective stuff."

"If Brunanski doesn't make it, it'll be homicide stuff," she said. "But we won't know for a while. What if the kid makes a run for it in the meantime? Let me go after this one. I promised I'd catch these assholes."

"Promised who?"

"Brunanski."

That shut Murphy up for a little while. He coughed and turned away, staring at the museum entrance. Three policemen were methodically screening the partygoers, patting them down for concealed weapons or works of art and asking questions.

"Okay," he said at last. "I've got your back on this one. But you let me know what you find, and we have to keep the detective bureau in the loop. You can run down your hunch. What do you need from me?"

"I need the kid's address," she repeated. "I need to see the security-camera footage from the museum. And I need the mailing tube."

"What for?"

"The man who was carrying it wasn't wearing gloves," she said.

"Cardboard won't take a print," he reminded her. "And there's probably not enough skin cells for DNA."

"It's not for me," she said with a grim smile. "It's for my partner. It'll smell like the perp."

"That tube is evidence," Murphy said.

"So get it taken to our precinct."

"This is 107's jurisdiction," he said. "It's their case. The only reason I'm here is because of Brunanski."

"Screw them!" Erin said. "Brunanski's one of ours. What was he doing here, anyway?"

"He was working traffic near the 495 exits, just happened to be in the area," Murphy said, shaking his head. "Okay, I'll take it up with Lieutenant Barnes and see what I can do."

While they were talking, information began to pour in from the network of officers combing the area around Flushing Meadows. The Corolla had turned up right away, just off the Grand Central Parkway entrance ramp, but it was abandoned. The car itself had been stolen, just as Erin suspected, three weeks prior, its plates switched with another car's, so vehicle registration would be a dead end. The perps had doubtless changed to another vehicle. But they'd left something behind.

"The car has three bullet holes in the bodywork and a broken window," the officer on scene reported over the radio.

"Four out of six," Murphy said to Erin with a smile. "Pretty good shooting at that range."

"Bloodstains on the back seat upholstery," the officer continued.

A low, angry cheer, almost a growl, went up from the police who heard the radio report. Several of them clapped Erin on the back.

The BOLO was immediately updated to note that at least one of the suspects had been wounded. Hospitals in the area were notified.

Murphy conferred briefly with Barnes, the lieutenant from the 107. After their conversation, he came back to where Erin waited.

"Okay, we've got an understanding," he said. "Barnes is letting us run with this one, on one condition."

Erin raised an eyebrow and crossed her arms.

"When we, and I quote, 'catch those cop-shooting pieces of shit, kick their asses so hard they taste patent leather.'" Murphy delivered the line deadpan, with no hint of humor.

"Can do, sir," Erin said.

"All right. Get in uniform as soon as you're ready," Murphy said. "We'll have the evidence back at the 116 by midnight. You may want to catch some sleep in the meantime."

"Later," she said. "I want to brace Huntington tonight. While he's asleep will be the best chance to nab him at home."

"You going to arrest him?" Murphy asked.

"I'm the least of his problems," she said.

* * *

Erin's hunch was that Cal was a patsy, not a full member of the gang. Otherwise they wouldn't have left him behind at the store. But she might be wrong. Hell, the thieves might be at Cal's place that very moment, lying low.

That was the last place a group of gunmen would be likely to go, of course. With a wounded comrade and every police officer in Queens looking for them, would they really hang out at the home of an associate who was out on bail? They had to assume the NYPD would be all over Cal. And they would be, as soon as the connection between him and the art thieves became known at the precinct.

She had to hurry, and not because she was in a race with the other cops. She had to get to Cal before he found out about the shootout. She hoped he hadn't known the particulars of the heist, especially its timing, because if he had, he'd already be in hiding. But if he saw a news item about a bunch of crooks dressed as security guards, it wouldn't matter what else he knew. He'd run. And she didn't have a car. So she had to swallow her pride.

Luke was standing quietly off to one side, watching the police going about their business. Erin walked toward him with more confidence than she felt.

"Luke?"

"Erin," he replied noncommittally.

"Listen, I was rude back there, and I'm sorry," she said. She paused, watching his reaction.

He managed a thin smile. "You were upset," he said. "I get it. And I didn't mean to get in the way. I just want to help."

"Good," Erin said. "Because there's something you can do."

He raised an eyebrow. "With all these cops here?"

"They're busy. I need a ride."

"Now?" He was confused. "I thought you were going after the criminals."

"Dressed like this?" Erin replied. "I need my shield and gun. So what do you say?"

He nodded. "I'll get the car."

Luke drove like a man who knew his car was expensive. He came to complete stops. He looked carefully at each intersection. He scrupulously obeyed all traffic regulations, including speed limits. It drove Erin crazy.

"I'm a cop," she said. "It's okay to go five over. I promise, I will not write you a ticket."

"I'd be surprised if you had your summons book tucked away," he said. "But I like to be careful. Driving is the most dangerous thing most people do most of the time."

"You don't need to tell me that," she retorted. "I'm an NYPD patrol officer. I respond to car crashes all the time. But I was in a gunfight earlier this evening, so right now I don't give a shit. Step on it."

He still drove cautiously, but he did speed up a little. "What happens after I get you home?" he asked as they headed east on the Long Island Expressway.

"You go home," she said, "and I go to work."

"Do you know who these guys are?"

"I will," she promised. "I've got a lead."

"Isn't it dangerous? Shouldn't you have... what do you call it, backup?"

According to the NYPD, Cal Huntington was a low-level crook, a burglar who'd been busted trying to crack a cash register for a lousy few twenties. But he was affiliated with a gang of gunmen who'd just stolen a priceless painting and shot a cop, and that meant going to see him alone was flat-out stupid. Damn right she should have backup.

"I'll have my partner," she said.

"Your *dog*?" He shook his head. "I don't like it."

"I needed a chauffeur, not a babysitter," Erin snapped.

"Has it ever occurred to you," Luke said, "that I might be saying this stuff because I like you and I don't want you to get hurt? Isn't one officer in the hospital enough for one night?"

"I'll be surprised if Brunanski makes it to the hospital," Erin said in a much lower voice.

"What do you mean?" Luke said.

"He took one in the liver," she said, "and he'd lost a lot of blood by the time the medics got to him. It's three-to-one that he's already dead."

"Jesus," Luke swore softly.

"So spare me the protective bullshit," she said. "I know what's on the line. Yes, I think it's sweet that you don't want me to get killed. I'll call you after, let you know I'm okay."

"I'd appreciate that," Luke said. Erin glanced at him and saw that he really did seem to mean it. "Here we are," he said, pulling up outside her apartment.

She leaned across the seat and gave him a quick kiss on the cheek. "Thanks," she said. Then she jumped out of the car, high heels dangling from one hand, and scampered across the concrete.

Chapter 8

With her uniform on her back, her Glock on her hip, and her dog at her side, Erin felt much better. She had a job to do, and as long as she focused on that, she could push her memories to the back of her mind. She knew she'd be seeing Brunanski's sheet-white face, and feeling the warmth of his blood seeping through her fingers, for a long time to come. But not tonight.

She picked up her squad car from the precinct motor pool. This was technically against regulations, as she wasn't on duty, but Lieutenant Murphy had given her permission, so no one was going to say anything about it. She drove the Charger as unobtrusively as she could. No flashing lights, no sirens.

The Huntington residence was a brick duplex on 165th, a couple of blocks from the uniform store. Erin pulled up to the house two doors down. She didn't want to give him time to run for it. She checked her watch. It was quarter past two. That was both good and bad. Cal was probably home, asleep, but according to his file, he lived with Mom and Dad, so his parents were there, too. They'd be a complication.

She took a few moments to case the house, making a quick walk-around. Most of the lights were off, but a glow came from one of the ground-floor windows. She stepped close to the window and peered around the edge of the shade.

Cal Huntington was at his computer, a pair of headphones clamped to his skull, completely oblivious to the outside world.

Erin sighed. A movie cop would break the window and haul Cal's sorry ass out into the street, or kick in the door with all the righteous fury of the NYPD. She couldn't do any of those things, not if she still wanted to have her shield come Monday morning. She needed probable cause or a warrant in order to enter a private residence without permission.

Constrained by the rules of civilized behavior, she did the only thing she could. She went to the front door and rang the bell.

She had to ring three times, waiting a half-minute between attempts, before an upstairs light signaled that one of the older Huntingtons had crawled out of bed. A short while later, the bulb over the doorstep flicked on. Erin stood with her back straight, doing her best to look every inch the tough, businesslike cop. Rolf, at her side, kept his ears perked forward and his long, intense face focused on the door.

Erin had found that the uniform could be either a blessing or a curse in situations like this. Most New Yorkers would hesitate to open their doors to a stranger in the middle of the night, but an officer could at least have a conversation across the chain of a night-lock. But lots of citizens, law-abiding or not, weren't too fond of the police.

Mr. Huntington, eyes bleary, graying hair sticking out at odd angles, opened the door and blinked at her. He was wearing striped pajamas, an old bathrobe, and brown fuzzy slippers.

"Officer? What's the matter?" he asked.

"I need to talk to Calvin," Erin said.

Wakeful wariness came into Mr. Huntington's face. "Oh, no," he said. "Not without a lawyer. You people have gotten him in enough trouble already."

"It's nothing like that," Erin said. "He's not the one in trouble. In fact, we need his help. If he can give us some information, it'll stand him in good stead. I may be able to get the charges against him dropped."

She saw the sudden hope in Cal's father's eyes. Her gut twisted in self-disgust at manipulating a parent's emotions. But not only was it necessary, it was also true. If Cal gave up the museum thieves, Erin was sure the D.A. would agree that tossing out the burglary charge was a more than fair trade.

"All right," Mr. Huntington said. "Come on in."

Erin and Rolf trooped into the house. Its furnishings were worn, but the home was neat and well-kept. It was your basic middle-class Queens family residence.

The door to the den was closed, light seeping under it. Mr. Huntington paused outside. "I'm afraid I'm going to have to insist on being present," he said. "You understand, I'm sure?"

"Perfectly," Erin said, managing to only grit her teeth a little. She needed to play hardball with the kid, and that was going to be more difficult with his dad as referee. Cal was over eighteen, so there was no legal requirement for another adult to be present. Still, Mr. Huntington didn't strike her as a particularly hard case. Things might work out anyway.

Cal barely glanced up as his father opened the door. He returned his attention to his computer screen. Then, as his brain caught up with his glimpse of Erin's face just behind his dad, he did a classic double-take. His eyes widened in a look of dismay that would have been comical in other circumstances.

Erin moved past Mr. Huntington before he could get in her way, crossing the room in five quick strides. Rolf kept pace with her. Sensing her mood, the dog raised his hackles and emitted a low, rumbling growl.

Cal started to get out of his swivel chair. Erin clamped her hands on the arms of the chair, trapping him in place. She swung the seat to face her head-on. As the kid stared up at her, she raised her left hand and snatched off his headphones.

"Evening, Calvin," she said in a dangerously quiet voice.

"Oh, man," he said. "Not you again."

"Listen to me very carefully, Calvin," Erin said, leaning close so that her face was only a few inches from his. "I'm going to ask you some questions, and you're going to answer them. You got that?"

"Hey, I don't have to say anything," he protested. "My lawyer said—"

"Your lawyer didn't say anything about protecting cop-killers," Erin snapped.

"Cop what now?" Cal blurted, his face showing genuine confusion.

Mr. Huntington stepped hesitantly forward. "Listen, ma'am, I don't think you can just—" he started to say.

Erin didn't let him finish. "Your friends, Calvin, the ones you helped steal those uniforms, just shot a police officer. You know what that makes you?"

He started to say something, but it had been a rhetorical question. She rode right over him. "It makes you an accessory to murder. You helped them set it up. That means you did it, too."

She doubted the jury would see it quite that way, but that wasn't the point. Cal needed to see it that way. She needed him to be scared. Looking into his eyes, less than a foot away from her own, she saw what she wanted. Now it was time to dangle a little hope, see if he went for it. "You were protecting your friends, and I respect that. But this is a lot more serious now. I don't think you knew what was going to happen, Cal. Jake just told you it was a little harmless fun and profit. Isn't that what happened?"

He grabbed at the line she'd given him and hung on like a drowning man. "Yeah!" he said eagerly. "It was just a prank, really. He didn't say nothing about anyone getting hurt. You gotta believe me!"

"I believe you, Cal," she said, "but you're going to have to convince more than just me. Your buddy Jake shot a police officer. He's going to prison for the rest of his life. Do you want to go with him?"

"He's not my buddy!" Cal protested. "I know him, sure, but we're not, like, friends!"

"Where do you know him from?" Erin demanded, leaning in still closer.

"Around! I don't know! He's just this guy, you know?" The kid's eyes darted wildly. His father edged closer, but didn't intervene.

"You can do better than that," Erin snapped. "Where does he live?"

"An apartment on 164th, just across Union Turnpike!" Cal said.

"What's his full name?"

"Gallagher. Jake Gallagher." The kid kept shrinking back into his chair.

Erin straightened up. "Good. That's good, Cal. Now, Jake had some friends with him tonight. Three other guys. Do you know the names of any of the guys he hangs out with? Guys who might have helped him out?"

"Well, there's Randy, and Mike, and maybe Joey," Cal said, relaxing a little now that Erin wasn't in his face.

"Do Randy, Mike, and Joey have last names?"

"I don't know them real well," he said.

Erin took a deep breath. "Okay, thank you, Calvin," she said. "You're being a big help. If you can give me just a little more, I'll be on my way. I want you to think carefully. What do these guys look like?"

Cal thought it over. "Randy's tall and real skinny, like six-two or something, with a sketchy beard and messy, curly hair. Black hair."

Erin mentally ticked off one of the two guards who had held the fake criminal during the heist. He'd been tall and thin, but he'd apparently shaved off the goatee and combed his hair for the occasion. "Go on," she said.

"Joey's a little dude, kinda mean-looking. He's got some ink he's proud of, a tattoo of a chick on his chest."

"When you say chick, you mean...?" Erin prompted.

Cal looked at his dad and squirmed a little. "A naked girl."

"Okay, good," she said. "And Mike?"

"Mike's crazy," Cal said. "He's always getting into fights, loves to talk about all the guys he's fu—I mean, messed up. He's really strong, into the whole weightlifting thing."

Erin nodded. The other guard who'd held the hapless museum patron had been very muscular. "This Mike, does he have a shaved head, like Jake?"

"Yeah!" Cal exclaimed. "And crazy eyes. Bright blue, and they look right past you when he's talking to you."

"Okay, Calvin," Erin said. She'd pulled out her hip notebook and scribbled a few quick notes. "Thanks for your cooperation. I'll need you to come in to the precinct and sign a statement. You do that, and I'll see what I can do about your little burglary problem." She turned to Mr. Huntington. "Sir, thank you. You've helped the NYPD, but you've also helped your son. I'm sorry for disturbing your sleep. I'll be going now, and let you get back to bed."

Mr. Huntington escorted her to the door with the same weak, half-hearted manner he'd displayed the whole time. Erin wanted to smack him. If he'd shown a little more authority when his kid was growing up, she thought, maybe Cal wouldn't be running around with guys like Jake and Mike.

As soon as she was out of the house, she jogged to her car and picked up the radio. "Dispatch, this is O'Reilly, four-six-four-oh. I need an address on a Jake Gallagher, near 164th and Union Turnpike," she said.

After a moment, the answer came: "78-34 164th, Apartment 301."

"Okay. I need any available officers. I've got a tip on the location on one of the museum shooters."

Erin was all in favor of going it alone, but she wasn't about to barge in on an apartment that might be full of armed, desperate men. For this, she was definitely going to want more backup than her dog.

* * *

Erin got to the apartment first, since she was already en route, but other officers arrived quickly afterward. Half a dozen squad cars converged on the building from all directions. Police threw up a cordon around the site, setting barricades at either end of the block. The officers double-checked their body armor and pumped shells into their shotguns. There was none of the usual banter. Their faces were hard and intense.

She buckled Rolf into his K-9 bulletproof vest, press-checked her Glock to ensure a round was chambered, and looked for the officer in command. It was Sergeant Daniels, a lean, quiet man from Harlem. Erin was glad to see him. Daniels was a good man in a crisis.

"O'Reilly," he said, catching sight of her. "You called this in?"

"Yeah," she replied. "I got a tipoff from an associate. Suspect's name is Gallagher, Jake or Jacob. Six-two, maybe six-three, muscular, shaved head, with a tattoo of a snake on his right arm. There may be up to three others, Randy, Mike, and Joey. Randy's tall and skinny, Mike's got a shaved head and is bulky like Gallagher, and Joey's small, with a tattoo of a naked girl on his chest."

Daniels looked closely at her. "Is this information good?"

"I think so," she said. "I braced an accomplice from a burglary. The descriptions match the guys I saw at the museum tonight."

"You were there?" he asked, surprised. "You see it go down?"

She nodded. "I can ID the suspects."

"Excellent." Daniels motioned to five nearby officers. "Circle up. I heard from Dispatch. ESU's not available. They're downtown, on another mission, could take hours. We're going in, apartment 301. Stewart, you lead with the sledgehammer. Once you breach, the rest of us go in. Paulson, then me, then Giametti, Ramirez, and Cox. O'Reilly, you follow up with your K-9. We clear the apartment and detain everybody inside. Once we've secured it, I want O'Reilly to sweep the place with the dog. Make sure we get everyone and everything there."

He gave them a grim look. "These guys already shot one cop tonight. Make sure no one else gets hit. Remember, we're here to do our job, not for revenge. Don't go in shooting, but if a guy goes for a weapon, or if you take fire, you put these bastards on the ground. Got it?"

There were nods and murmurs of assent all round.

"Okay," Daniels said. "Let's do this."

The apartment building was red brick, with a wrought-iron fence running along the sidewalk. The breaching team entered through the parking lot and made their way through the lobby. They called the elevators down to the main floor, another officer holding them there. The team went up the stairs, guns raised and ready. The time was three in the morning and the complex was dead silent. They met no one in the stairwell or hallway.

Officer Stewart, a brawny guy with a bushy mustache, hefted his sledgehammer. He nodded to Paulson, a small, wiry man who'd been an Army Ranger before joining the NYPD. Paulson rapped sharply on the door.

"Open up! NYPD!"

They gave it two seconds, and then Stewart swung the hammer in a sideways arc. The doorframe splintered, the lock smashing straight through the flimsy woodwork. The door swung open. Paulson was inside in an instant, shotgun poised, clearing the vulnerable doorway. Daniels was right behind him.

Erin, standing at the back, fumed impatiently. She wanted to be up front. She watched one officer after another rush into the apartment, heard the shouts of "Living room clear!" "Bathroom clear!" and "Bedroom clear!" Then it was her turn. She and Rolf lunged into the apartment.

It was anticlimactic. Policemen emerged from various doorways, shaking their heads. Stewart slammed his fist against the wall in frustration. "No one here, Sarge," he growled.

"Okay, search the place," Daniels said. "Be thorough, people. Paulson, watch the hallway."

Erin turned Rolf loose with the single German word "*Such,*" giving him his "search" command. The dog put his nose to the old, worn carpet and made a full examination of the area. When he was finished, he turned to Erin, sat, and cocked his head. He was trained to search for people and explosives, and he'd found neither.

She fought back her disappointment. For just a moment, she'd thought the solution would be easy. She'd pictured the police bursting in on the stunned criminals, sweeping up the whole gang at one go. She'd let herself imagine a commendation from Lieutenant Murphy. While the others began searching the bedroom, closet, and living room, she went into the bathroom and stared at herself in the mirror.

The reflection of a red-eyed, utterly exhausted woman stared back. She'd been on the go for what felt like days. Her emotions were balanced on a ragged edge of raw nerves. She closed her eyes and clenched her hands. In her helpless anger, she nearly punched the bathroom mirror.

Proper crime-scene procedure stopped her hand mid-motion. She wasn't supposed to touch anything without gloves, and she certainly wasn't supposed to break anything. As she paused to retrieve a pair of latex gloves from a pocket of her vest, the habitual action put her mind in evidence-collecting mode. She tried to pull herself together, to get through the task in front of her.

Still staring at the mirror, she stretched the gloves over her hands and pulled, revealing the medicine cabinet. It was mostly empty, with just the sort of meds she'd expect to find in a bachelor's pill compartment: Aspirin, antacid, shaving cream, a disposable razor, and a couple prescription bottles. She picked up one of these and squinted at the lettering printed on the side. It was a bottle of Vicodin, prescribed by a Dr. Boland at Queens Hospital and dated the week before last.

What did that mean? Jake was probably either at a hideout, or with one of his friends. Where would a criminal go, when he had a wounded comrade?

"Sarge!" she called, feeling a hint of her previous excitement.

Daniels appeared in the doorway. "What've you got?" he asked.

"Pain pills," she said, showing him the bottle. "Prescription stuff."

"You think he's a junkie?" he asked, examining the bottle.

"Maybe," Erin said. "But mostly what I was thinking is, if he's got a crooked doc who slips him these happy pills, that might be who he'd go see if one of his pals got hurt."

Daniels snapped his fingers. "Bingo," he said, grinning. "Good thought, O'Reilly. Call the hospital. We'll have guys from the Bureau check it out ASAP."

"I can go right down there," Erin suggested. "We don't have to wait. It's practically across the street."

"You're not a detective, O'Reilly," Daniels said. "Let's pass this one up the chain."

"Murphy said I could follow through on this," she argued. "Let me do this, Sarge."

Giametti knocked on the doorframe. "Hey, guys," he said. "This just came in over the net. Brunanski didn't make it."

"Shit," Daniels said, shaking his head. "God damn it!"

In her mind, Erin was back at Brunanski's squad car. *Keep talking, Brunanski, you ugly Polack. Stay with me.* She felt as if she'd been kicked in the stomach. For a second the bathroom swam in front of her eyes, and she thought she was going to throw up.

"O'Reilly? O'Reilly!"

She looked up at Daniels. The room came back in focus.

"This is now officially a homicide," he said. "It's their case. We're just beat cops. We do the grunt work. Let's get this info to them. It may be just what they need."

"I was holding him, Sarge," she said. "I felt him bleeding. Sure, go on, tell Homicide. They can do whatever the hell they want with this. But unless you order me to stand down, I'm going to the damn hospital now."

Daniels sighed. "I hope you know what you're doing, girl," he said. "You screw this up, it's gonna bite you right in the ass."

"I screw this up, an ass-chewing from Homicide is going to be the least of my worries," she shot back. "See you around,

Sarge." She took out her notebook, scribbled down the prescription number, whistled to Rolf, and left.

Chapter 9

As Erin steered her car down 164th, a wave of fatigue hit her so hard that she almost drove straight into a lamppost. She'd fired at criminals, tried to save a fellow cop's life, interrogated a small-time crook, stormed an apartment, and driven all over central Queens. She was wiped out.

But she couldn't stop yet. Not as long as she had a lead to follow. She'd promised Brunanski, and now Brunanski was dead, and you just did not break a promise to a dying man. Erin was going to see this through.

The hospital was just a few blocks south. She steered the Charger into the emergency-room lot, parked in one of the reserved police spaces, and got out, leaving Rolf in the car.

Most places were quiet at half past three in the morning, but not a New York emergency room. Erin stepped into a scene of controlled chaos. People were holding bloody towels over wounds. Elderly folks were there, supported by family members, with chest pains, slipped disks, and all the other hazards of age. A distraught mother holding a very small child in her arms was shouting at a harried-looking nurse. In the middle of it all, nurses and hospital staff tried to sort through the incoming patients to process the most serious cases first.

Erin had been in ERs dozens of times in the course of her Patrol duties. She ignored the bustle of the place. As she crossed the room, she caught sight of two other officers against the wall. They were from her precinct. One was a fellow female officer, Porter. The other was Mortensen, her partner.

"Hey! O'Reilly!" Porter called. She was a smart, tough black woman. She and Erin were on friendly terms, though not precisely friends. What they shared was mutual respect.

"Hey, Porter, Mortensen," Erin said, making her way through the crowd. "You hear about Brunanski?"

"Yeah," Mortensen said, giving her a funny look. "We've been in the chapel. A lot of the guys are there."

Belatedly, Erin realized that of course Brunanski had been brought to Queens Hospital. The building would be crawling with cops. Whenever an officer was wounded, his or her brethren would crowd into the hospital to keep vigil. Hell, there were probably some Homicide Division guys already on site.

"I didn't see you there," Porter said. "Did you just get in?"

"Yeah," Erin said, not wanting to take the time to explain. "Listen, I've got a lead. I gotta run."

"It about the shooting?" Porter asked.

Erin nodded.

"Go get 'em, girl," Porter said. "You need us, just holler."

Erin worked her way to the reception desk, cutting in line with no hesitation whatsoever, ignoring the protests of the waiting patients.

The nurse behind the desk gave her a tired stare. "What is it, Officer?"

"I need to speak with Dr. Boland," Erin said. "Is he on tonight?"

The woman didn't need to check the roster. "He's in surgery," she said. "He's in OR three right now, prepping for an appie."

"Thanks," Erin said, hurrying out of the waiting room. She knew the hospital pretty well, and only needed to consult the map by the elevator for a second in order to get her bearings. She got to the operating room and saw that she was just in time. The doctor, accompanied by a couple of nurses and an intern, were just finishing scrubbing their hands outside the OR. If she'd been a few moments later, they'd already be working.

"Dr. Boland!" she called.

The doctor was a mild-looking, gray-haired man in his mid-fifties, not at all the sort of guy she pictured slipping pills to a thug like Jake. He looked her over with faint surprise, taking in her uniform and unkempt condition. "Officer. I'm sorry, but I'm about to go into surgery. Perhaps we can talk later? My patient has acute appendicitis, and time really is of the essence in such cases."

"I just need a second, sir," Erin said. She pulled out the paper on which she'd copied the prescription from the medicine cabinet. "I need to know about Jake Gallagher."

"Who?"

Erin was well schooled in initial reactions. She was used to the reflexive lies perps told. She was watching the doctor carefully for all the usual telltales of surprise, fear, and dishonesty, but she didn't see anything but genuine lack of comprehension.

"Jake Gallagher," she repeated. "A big guy, shaved head, tattoo on his arm. You wrote him a prescription for Vicodin, two weeks ago."

"Young lady," Dr. Boland said, "I did no such thing."

"You're sure?" Erin pressed.

"I am quite certain," he said. "I have written sixteen Vicodin prescriptions in the past month, and I remember the names of every man, woman, and child. Jake Gallagher is not among them. If you have any doubts, inquire of Nurse Wright at the nurses' station. Now, if you have no further questions, I really must be about the business of saving a young man's life."

Erin let him go, momentarily stumped. Lacking a better idea, she did as he had suggested and went to the nurses' station.

"Nurse Wright?" she asked the heavyset woman behind the desk. The nurse's hair was a bright red that had certainly come out of a bottle.

"Yeah, hon? What's the matter?" the nurse replied.

"I need to see a prescription record," she said, handing over the slip of paper with the prescription info.

"You got a warrant?" Wright asked. "That's personal health information."

"I just spoke with Dr. Boland," Erin said smoothly. "He's gone into surgery, but he told me to double-check the prescription with you. I don't need any personal details. I just need to know whether Dr. Boland actually wrote this prescription. You don't even have to tell me what it's for, or in whose name."

The nurse sighed. "I guess that's all right," she said. "Give it here, hon." Taking the paper from Erin, she typed the number into her computer. Then there was a long, quiet moment.

"Huh," Nurse Wright said. "That's funny."

"How do you mean?" Erin asked, leaning forward on the desk and fighting the urge to sneak a peek at the computer screen.

"It's in Dr. Boland's name, signed for on May 25th."

"Why is that funny?"

"Dr. Boland was in Tampa at a conference the last week of May."

Erin felt a thrill of excitement, displacing her weariness. "You know that for a fact?"

"I filed his receipts, hon," the nurse said. "Expense accounts."

"So someone forged his signature," Erin said.

"Looks that way," the nurse said. "You a Narc?"

"Not exactly," Erin said. "Jake Gallagher, the guy this prescription was for, is a wanted fugitive. I need to know anything you can tell me about him." She described him for what seemed like the tenth time that night.

"Well, hon, I've never been properly introduced to the man, but he sounds like Sylvia's boyfriend."

"Sylvia?"

"I shouldn't gossip," the nurse said in the tones of every gossipy woman on the face of the earth, "but I always thought he was trouble. That boy looks like a born criminal."

"Who is Sylvia, please?" Erin persisted.

"Sylvia Paxton. She works here. Nurses' assistant."

"Does she work with Dr. Boland?"

"Of course."

"I don't suppose she's on duty tonight?"

"No, hon."

Erin sagged.

"She was supposed to come on duty at ten, but she called in sick," Nurse Wright continued.

Erin's head snapped up. "Was she at the hospital on the 25th? Did she have access to write prescriptions?"

"Let me check the schedule," the nurse said. "Hmm... let's see... yes. She worked nine to five that day, lucky girl."

"I need her address," Erin said. "Right now."

* * *

"Whose address?"

Erin spun. Two men had come up behind her. Despite the lateness, or earliness, of the hour, they were immaculately groomed, clean-shaven, and wearing pressed suits and ties. She recognized them at once. The tall, broad-shouldered one was Detective Lyons, and the short, pudgy one was Detective Spinelli. They were part of Precinct 116's Homicide unit.

"Detectives," Erin said. "You're up early."

"And you're up late, O'Reilly," Lyons said. "What're you doing in uniform? You're off duty."

"Don't you Homicide boys have better things to do than check duty rosters?" Erin replied, but her heart sank. If they knew her work schedule, it meant they were checking up on her, personally. She thought of Rolf, and how she liked to let him run free at the dog park. Her own brief run off-leash was coming to an end.

"As a matter of fact, we do," Spinelli said. "We investigate homicides. Like that of John Brunanski."

"Shouldn't you be home in bed, O'Reilly? You look tired." A look of entirely false concern was on Lyons's face.

Weariness and irritation wore away some of Erin's manners and better judgment. "Lay off me, guys. I'm just doing my job."

"Looks to me like you're trying to do our job," Spinelli corrected her. "We hear you've been running all over Queens, busting down doors, interrogating suspects..."

"Like a detective," Lyons interjected.

"Which you're not," Spinelli finished. "So run along. You don't have to go home if you don't want to..."

"Why not write some parking tickets?" Lyons suggested.

"...But leave this to us," Spinelli said. "We're trained for this sort of thing. And we're fresh. You're about to keel over. Let us handle this, girl. You've carried the ball; now hand it off to us, and we'll run with it."

"Into the end zone," Lyons added.

Calling her "girl," then going straight into the football metaphors, Erin thought. Could the macho bullshit be any thicker? Her jaw tightened. "Okay, you're the hotshot Homicide dicks," she said. "And you're right, I'm just a beat cop. What the hell do I know? You're right, I'm going home."

"Whose address were you asking about?" Spinelli demanded.

"Ask her," Erin retorted.

"Withholding information in a murder investigation?" Spinelli said.

"That's a serious thing," Lyons said.

Erin's temper finally got the better of her. "Okay, assholes," she snapped. "Sylvia Paxton is a nurse here. She's the girlfriend of one of the suspects and I'm guessing she's with him, probably at her place. Why? 'Cause he's been shot. That's because I shot him after he and his buddies tagged one of ours. She forged a Vicodin prescription for one of the suspects. You know all this because I went and got the info while you were screwing around with your thumbs up your asses. But hell, I'm not trained for this, so it's probably all bullshit, right? So I'm out of here."

Lyons's face flushed and he took a step toward her, flexing his hands. "You think I won't kick your ass just because you're a girl?"

"I think you won't kick my ass because I'd wipe the floor with you," Erin shot back.

Lyons, eight inches taller than Erin and outweighing her by eighty pounds, growled low in his throat. He took another step forward. Erin, a shot of adrenaline pushing back her fatigue, dropped into a judo stance. Even wide awake and fresh, she'd have been no match for him in a fistfight, but right then she didn't care.

"Whoa, whoa," Spinelli said, stepping between his partner and Erin. He held his hands out. "Okay, you know what, O'Reilly? You've done a good job tonight. Really, a hell of a job. But this is our case now. You don't like it, I get that. And I respect that. Why don't you take it up with Murphy when the sun comes up? Right now, we've got a job to do. You want to get the guys who shot Brunanski, so do we. You've helped. But now, go home."

Erin was still furious. She wanted to hit something. Specifically, she wanted to hit Lyons. But she realized, as the heat of the moment cooled down, she mostly wanted to hit Jake and his gang. She was too tired. She wasn't thinking straight. And damn it all, that meant the Homicide boys were at least a little bit right.

"Okay," she sighed. Then she made eye contact with Lyons, who was still glowering at her. "I'll see you around."

She left the hospital without looking back. Getting into her car, she drove carefully home. She'd responded to enough traffic accidents to know that fatigue caused as many wrecks as drunk driving. She put her radio on to a hard-rock station and turned the air conditioning up so it blasted icy air straight into her face. Somehow, she got back to her apartment without running into anything. She took Rolf for a quick turn around the block to do his business, then headed upstairs, stripped off her uniform, and collapsed into bed. The time was a little before five o'clock, and the sun would be coming up much too soon.

Chapter 10

Erin woke to the ring of her phone. She blinked, tried to sit up, and flailed at her nightstand. The phone spun to the floor. Still groggy, her head aching, she scrambled out of bed and fumbled the device into her hands, just in time for it to stop ringing.

She brought up the call history and saw she'd missed two other calls from the same number... Luke's number. Erin swore softly. She'd promised to call him after things calmed down, but running from one lead to the next, she'd blanked it out. She checked the time and swore again. It was ten-thirty. Fortunately, she wasn't on the duty roster for Saturday, but she hadn't meant to sleep so late.

Erin returned the call. The phone rang only once before Luke's agitated voice came on the line.

"Erin? Are you okay?"

She sighed. "Yeah, Luke, I'm fine. Look, I'm sorry I didn't call before. I didn't get back to my place until almost five, and then I was so tired... anyway, like I said, I'm fine."

"I'm glad to hear it," Luke replied, but his voice was still tight with worry and the anger that came with it. But he was trying to be a good guy, so he kept talking, quiet and calm. "I read about the other officer. I'm sorry."

She closed her eyes and clenched her jaw. "Me, too," she said. "It wasn't exactly a surprise. He was hit pretty bad."

Luke paused. "So, did you find them?" he asked after a respectful moment.

"Not yet," Erin said. "I think I found where one of them lives. And we've got some names."

"That's great!" he said with forced enthusiasm. "Sounds like you're closing in. Is there anything I can do?"

She was about to say no, but then a thought hit her. "You can take me to breakfast," she said. "There's something I'd like to ask you about."

"Okay, sure," Luke said. "I can be by in about half an hour."

*   *   *

They went to a diner down the street from Erin's apartment. Her headache had faded a little, and she felt like she hadn't eaten in days. She attacked a stack of pancakes, with fried eggs and bacon on the side. Luke contented himself with a cup of coffee and an English muffin. He watched in silent astonishment as she devoured her food.

"What's the matter?" she asked between mouthfuls. "You afraid I'll lose my girlish figure?"

He blinked. "Sorry," he said. "It's... impressive, is all."

"My dad ate like this every day of his life, I'll have you know," she said.

"And does he still have his girlish figure?" Luke asked with a raised eyebrow.

Erin thought of her father, all two hundred forty pounds of him. "No," she conceded. "But last night was a little unusual."

He looked closely at her. "You want to talk about it?"

"Not really," she said. "I want to talk about art."

"Art? Really?" he asked with undisguised surprise. "I thought you'd be all wrapped up in the case."

"And it's a case about art," she said. "It's not about Brunanski. He just got in the way. The point was swiping the Madonna. You know about art, Luke. Why steal that painting?"

"It's the most valuable piece in the collection," he said at once. "It's worth more than all the others put together, to the right buyer."

"But that's the problem, isn't it," Erin said. "Finding a buyer. That's why theft of really valuable art is so rare. Remember those guys in Norway who stole that painting? You know, the one with the guy clapping his hands to his face like the kid in *Home Alone*?"

"*The Scream*," Luke said. "Edvard Munch. There were two thefts, of two different versions of the painting."

"Really?" It was Erin's turn to be surprised.

"Yeah. The one from the Oslo National Gallery was stolen in '94, and the one from the Munch Museum was grabbed in '04. The first one was held for ransom, so the police faked a payment and arrested everybody. The second one sat around in hiding for two years, then was recovered."

"Whatever," she said. "My point is, they couldn't sell it. It was too famous."

"Everyone in the world knew it had been stolen," Luke agreed. "And no one got paid in the end."

"You know a lot about art theft," Erin said.

"In my line of work, you have to," he said. "Otherwise, I could be asked to appraise a painting that was stolen, and if I didn't know it, I'd be in trouble. I know a lot about market value, and by necessity, that includes what a given work could bring on the black market. I do a lot of research."

"That's what I figured," she said. "So why steal this painting, if it's impossible to sell?"

"The Madonna hasn't been officially authenticated," he said. "I was one of the experts preparing to do just that. The authentication was set to happen before the exhibit closed. Until that happens, legally speaking, it would be possible for a collector to buy the painting, sit on it for a while, and then reveal it."

"But there are pictures of it already," Erin said. "Everyone would know it was the same painting."

"They could argue this painting was a forgery, and they had the original it was copied from," Luke explained. "Only a few experts have seen the one that was taken, and there'd be no proof."

"Okay," Erin said. "So we know why it was taken now. Later on, once you and the other art guys vouched for it, it'd be too late to steal and auction."

"Do you know how rare it is for an undocumented work of a Renaissance master to be discovered?" Luke said. "This was a unique opportunity. The Madonna should never have been put on display before being authenticated, and the security should have been twice as strong."

"But it wasn't," Erin said. "So, Luke, what do you do once you've stolen the painting?"

He blinked. "You think *I* stole it?" he exclaimed.

Erin had to laugh. "No, I think if you were planning an art heist, you wouldn't have brought a cop along as your date. I meant, if you were to have this painting, and wanted to sell it, what would your next move be?"

"You can't peddle stolen art like a stolen TV set," Luke said. "I mean, it's not like you can just go on eBay and say, 'Hey, I've got a stolen Raphael Madonna, starting price thirty million, buy now for fifty million.'"

"*Fifty million?*" Erin echoed. "You're shitting me."

"No, I'm not," he said. "I may be underestimating. In 2012, a drawing by Raphael sold for 47.8 million dollars at a Sotheby's auction. That was for a black chalk drawing of an apostle's head, not even a finished painting. From his *sketchbook*. So you understand the stakes we're talking about here?"

She whistled softly. "Okay. Yeah. I get it. So how would you sell something like this?"

"Like I said, you can't do an online auction. Not without attracting all sorts of law-enforcement attention. And you can't go through the major auction houses. Back in the nineteenth century, they didn't much care if a work was stolen, but now? No reputable house would touch it. What I'd do, I'd have the buyer lined up ahead of time, before even stealing it."

"You think someone else put these guys up to the job?" Erin asked. "Hired them for it?"

"I'd bet on it," Luke said. "What do you know about the thieves?"

Erin shrugged. "They're small-time thugs, local boys."

"Where would guys like that get the idea to dress up like security guards and steal a specific painting?" he asked.

"They wouldn't," she said. "You think they knew how valuable it was?"

"Probably not," Luke said. "Why would their employer tell them?"

"I'm guessing they got offered a commission," Erin said, thinking out loud. "Five or six thousand, tops. You don't want to pay millions of dollars to street punks, even if you can afford it. They'll just buy fancy cars and start flashing handfuls of bills around, and the next thing you know, everyone starts asking questions."

He nodded. "That makes sense. Unfortunately, it also makes the pool of potential buyers pretty large. Plenty of people can afford five grand for a painting."

"Yeah, but how many of them are in Queens right now?"

"What do you mean?"

"Jake seems like the kind of guy who doesn't do business over the phone," she explained. "He did everything in person with the kid he got for the uniform-store heist. I'm pretty sure he's got his girlfriend taking care of the one that got wounded last night. I get the feeling he wouldn't pull a job like this without meeting the buyer. He'll do the handoff face-to-face if he can. That way he's sure to get paid."

"That narrows it down a bit," Luke said. "Is that what you wanted to ask me? Who would be interested in buying stolen paintings around here?"

"I don't care about the art black market," Erin said. "All I care about is who on that market would buy this particular painting, and would be willing to steal in order to get his hands on it."

"I can get you a list of names," Luke said. "But I don't know—"

Erin gave him her most dazzling smile. "Thanks, Luke," she said. "I knew I could count on you."

He shook his head. "Are you using me, Erin O'Reilly?" he asked.

Erin wiped her mouth, leaned across the table, and kissed him lightly on the lips. "What do you think?"

He smiled. "I think I could get used to it." His smile faded a little. "I really was worried about you last night."

"It's a dangerous job sometimes," she said. "But most crooks know better than to mix it up with the cops. It's not that bad."

"Erin, an officer got killed last night. He was standing right next to you."

"You think I don't know that?" she snapped, more sharply than she meant to. "That's rare," she added, bringing her tone of voice back down. "I'm careful and I'm good at my job. But it's nice to know you care."

"I do," he said.

"I appreciate it, Luke," she said. "If you could get me that list today, that'd be great. Now I've got to go to work."

"You're working today?" he asked, startled.

"Not officially," she admitted. "Officially, I'm off the case. But yeah, I'm working. I need to find out how badly those two jackasses from Homicide have screwed things up. Call me when you have those names, okay?"

"Sure thing, Officer," he said, touching his fingertips to his brow in a mock salute.

Erin stuck out her tongue at him as she slid out of the booth, surprising both of them with the girlish gesture. Then, impulsively, she leaned in and kissed him again. She lingered a moment, feeling the stubble on his chin against her face. Her lips parted slightly. She was surprised at how nice it felt. It had been a long time since she'd been this close to a man, and she'd almost forgotten the sensations it rekindled in her.

But there was work to do, and Erin didn't have the time or the emotional energy to spare, no matter how handsome and charming Luke Devins might be. "Catch you on the flip-side," she said, leaving the diner and heading back to her case.

* * *

Erin wasn't in uniform. She wasn't on duty. She'd been warned off the case by Homicide. She went to the station anyway. She had some evidence to pick up, and she wanted to see what had happened while she'd been asleep.

She should've checked the news first. TV vans and reporters were swarming all over the parking lot when she arrived. Erin knew better than to ask a reporter what had gone down, so she just walked straight into Precinct 116, Rolf trotting by her side, ignoring the press.

One of the first cops she ran into was Porter. Porter had gone off-duty and changed out of her uniform, but she was still hanging around the station. Erin found her by the coffee machine.

"Hey, Porter," she said. "What'd I miss?"

"Stick around for the press conference," Porter said dryly. "They've got 'em."

"What?" Erin exclaimed. "All of them?"

"Not quite," Porter admitted. "The Homicide guys called in ESU when they came available and made a raid just before eight this morning. They hit the apartment of some girl, the girlfriend of one of the gang. Nabbed two of them, plus the chick, of course."

Erin slammed her fist against the doorframe. She'd slept through the bust. Maybe the biggest case of her career, and Lyons and Spinelli had snatched it right out from under her. Plus, they'd screwed the pooch, just like she'd thought. "Just two?" she asked. "Who got away?"

"Gallagher, and one of his pals," Porter said. "You remember Wallace? I dated him for a while."

"Yeah, I know him," Erin said. "What about him?"

"He's on rotation to ESU, so he gave me some info," Porter said. "The area wasn't properly secured, he said. Gallagher and his buddy did a rabbit when ESU kicked in the door. Went out the bathroom window, down the fire escape, and then they lost 'em. Some shots got fired, but no one was hit."

"Why wasn't there a perimeter?" Erin demanded.

"Wallace said Spinelli was in a hurry, wanted to wrap the whole thing up in time for the morning news cycle. Wallace was some kind of pissed. He figures they blew their big chance at taking down the whole gang at once, and now there's a couple fugitives running scared, armed and dangerous, of course." Porter rolled her eyes.

"So they got the wounded guy, the nurse, and one of the others? Which one?"

"Tall, skinny guy. Randall, I think."

"Okay, thanks," Erin said. "I've gotta go." She hurried to Lieutenant Murphy's office.

She found Murphy in front of his mirror, adjusting his necktie. He turned startled eyes on her. "O'Reilly? What are you doing here?"

"I've come for the mailing tube," she said. "Can you sign it out to me?"

"Mailing tube?" he echoed.

"From the gallery?" Erin reminded him.

"Right! That mailing tube," he said. "It's down in Evidence. You hear we got two of them?"

"Yeah, and let two get away," she said.

Murphy shrugged. "Classic screw-up," he said. "Two of the blocking units couldn't get on station in time, and before they were in position, Spinelli went ahead with the breach. Now he's going to go in front of the cameras and claim it as a victory for law enforcement, which I guess it was."

"Sir, this was my case," she protested.

He laid a hand on her shoulder. "I said you could run with it," he said, not unkindly. "But it's a homicide now, and that takes it out of our hands. So what do you want to do? You want to be a detective?"

"Maybe I do," Erin said.

"I think you've got what it takes," Murphy said. "But we're a bureaucracy, it's a process, and right now, you're in Patrol Division. If you want, I can help get you on track for a gold shield. I'd hate to lose you. You're one of my best officers. But if that's what you want..."

"Sir, what I want right now is to make a clean sweep, get all these creeps before they kill someone else."

Murphy nodded. "Then get your dog to the corner of 164th and 77th. See if you can track them. That's why we've got the K-9s, isn't it?"

"Yes, sir!" Erin said. "Can I still have the mailing tube? It'll have scent on it."

"Sure thing," Murphy said. "I'll walk you down to Evidence. Then I've got to go to the press conference." He stood back at arm's length and gave her a long look. "How're you doing?"

"I'm okay, sir," she said.

"Fine. But take someone with you. If you do run into these guys, remember, they've already killed one of ours. Sergeant Daniels should be around somewhere. Ask him for Paulson or Stewart."

"Will do," she said. "Thanks, Lieutenant."

"You've got a window here," Murphy said. "The Homicide boys will be strutting in front of the cameras for an hour, and then they'll be sweating the perps. But don't think they're going to forget about you. Make Patrol proud. Get us a collar."

Erin started to leave.

"O'Reilly? One more thing."

She stopped, her hand on the doorknob.

"Anything feels hinky, you call for backup. No playing hero." Murphy wasn't smiling.

"No, sir."

"Okay, get your dog on the scent."

Chapter 11

Given the choice between the beefy Stewart and the wiry Paulson, Erin went with the little guy. It wasn't that she was intimidated by Stewart; quite the contrary. It was that Paulson was so scary that if Erin had to pick one guy in Precinct 116 to back her in a fight, it would be him. He'd been an Army Ranger and had served in Iraq. He'd been shot twice and blown clean out of a Humvee by a roadside bomb. He wasn't loud or outwardly violent. There was a quiet, dangerous air about him. When Erin told him she needed some backup, he just nodded and said, "Roger that."

Erin packed Rolf into his compartment and climbed behind the wheel of her Charger. Paulson rode shotgun. The target building was just a few minutes from the station. On the way, she explained what they were doing. Paulson had worked with K-9s, both overseas and with the NYPD, so he didn't need extra instruction.

"You think we'll find either of them?" he asked.

"I wouldn't be bringing you otherwise," she replied.

A pair of squad cars and the CSI van were still on-site at Sophie Paxton's apartment. One of the cops was leaning against the fender of his squad car, smoking. Erin freed Rolf and approached the patrolman. He nodded a greeting.

"Where'd the rabbits run off to?" she asked him.

"Down that way," the cop said, pointing with his half-smoked Marlboro to an arched passage that ran under the apartment. "We lost them in back of the building."

"Okay, thanks." Erin was holding a duffel bag which contained the infamous mailing tube, wrapped in brown paper to preserve the evidence. She put on a pair of gloves, opened the bag, and took out the tube. She held it in front of Rolf. "*Such*," she said.

The Shepherd sniffed the tube carefully and thoroughly. He raised his nose and tested the breeze. He bent down to the concrete, nostrils flaring. Then he was off, trotting briskly along the arched passageway, moving quickly in spite of his Kevlar vest.

Erin slung the duffel on her shoulder and followed, drawing her Glock and holding it by her side. A glance at her comrade told her that Paulson had retrieved the shotgun from the trunk of her squad car. He carried it like a soldier, stock against his shoulder, muzzle angled slightly down, index finger extended beside the trigger guard.

The two cops trailed the dog. Upon exiting the tunnel, Rolf turned sharply to the left. He came to a steel gate in a brick retaining wall, paused, and whined. Erin worked the latch and opened the door for him. Rolf slid through the opening and crossed 77th Road, headed north. The dog went up a driveway into a back yard, easing through a gap in the base of a wooden privacy fence. The hole was too small even for Erin. She and Paulson vaulted the fence into a yard. They quickly crossed the grass, exiting by another gate into a back alley.

Erin felt an excitement that was, on reflection, very optimistic. This trail was hours cold, and though Rolf was on a good scent, the chances of actually catching up to the fugitives were slim. They'd probably stolen a car, at which point the trail would end. Maybe, she dared hope, this would at least tell them what vehicle to look for.

Rolf continued through the middle of the block between 77th Road and 77th Avenue. Erin was continually surprised that the city planners would set up street names like that. They came to a makeshift fence of plywood panels. Above it she could see a half-built townhouse, nothing but a skeleton of bare wood with a roof and basic walls. Rolf whined again and scratched at the base of the fence.

"Over?" Erin wondered.

Paulson shook his head. "Around to the front. Pick up the trail at the door."

They circled the construction project to the street side. There, in the midst of a dozen warning signs and building permits, the workmen had incongruously fitted a house exterior door, complete with a stained-glass window in the center. Erin blinked at it and shook her head. Rolf paced back and forth on the sidewalk, sniffing and snorting, but his enthusiasm had been replaced by confusion. He'd lost the scent.

"Inside," Erin said, taking hold of the doorknob. She opened the door onto the packed dirt yard. Rolf and Paulson entered. Erin marveled at the similarity between them, man and dog moving with the same predatory purpose. The dog put his nose to the ground and immediately regained his confidence. He rushed to the base of a ladder which rested against the front wall of the building. Then he whined again and pawed at the bottom rung.

Erin pointed up the ladder. "You don't think..." she said very quietly.

Paulson's lips drew back in something that was almost a smile. "Bingo," he breathed.

Erin's hand strayed to the radio at her belt. Should she call for backup? They didn't know for a fact that anyone was here, and she'd already called in a tactical strike on an apartment that had proved to be empty. She thought of Lyons and Spinelli. What would they say? What would they do? She shook her head and left the radio where it was. Signaling to Paulson to stay at ground level, she went to the ladder and began to climb as quietly and carefully as she could, keeping her Glock in one hand.

It wasn't the sturdiest ladder. When she was about halfway up, it shifted against the side of the building. Wood creaked loudly. Erin froze, one foot poised, holding her breath.

Moments passed. Nothing happened.

She let out her breath slowly and took another step up. She ducked low. She didn't want to have her head exposed until she could bring up her gun to cover the second floor. She was facing a sheet of plywood which extended about half the height of the second story. She had no idea what was on the other side.

The faint metallic *click* wouldn't have meant much to a civilian, but Erin recognized the sound of a pistol's slide chambering a round. She froze again for a fraction of a second, weighing her options, then jumped off the ladder.

Even as she was airborne, she heard the gunshots, four shots in such rapid succession that she hadn't landed by the time the fourth bullet splintered the plywood exactly where she'd been.

She hit the hard-packed dirt with a jarring shock, her legs buckling at the impact. "Damn!" she grunted.

Paulson was already moving with the reflexes of a combat veteran. He didn't go up the ladder, or back off to get a better angle on the upper floor. He went into the unfinished house, through the gap where the front living-room window would be, so he was standing directly beneath the room from which the shots had come. Pointing the shotgun at the ceiling, he fired straight up. The twelve-gauge buckshot tore through the thin subfloor. He pumped the shotgun, stepped to one side, fired again, then a third time.

"Okay! Okay! Jesus Christ!"

The cry, more frightened than injured, came from the second floor. Paulson, unmoved by the plea to his lord and savior, pumped another shell into his Remington and sent a fourth shell through the ceiling in the direction of the voice.

"This is the NYPD! Throw the gun down!" Erin shouted. She held her finger tight on the Glock's trigger, aiming up.

After a long moment, a Sig-Sauer automatic was hurled over the side of the second floor to land in the dirt with a thud.

"Come down!" Erin called. "I'd better see your hands, and they'd better be in the air!"

"I can't!" came the panicky response. "I'm hurt! I'm shot!"

"Where?" she demanded.

"In the legs! I'm bleeding! Oh shit, I'm gonna die!"

Paulson shook his head in disgust. "Call for backup," he muttered.

Erin grabbed her radio. "Dispatch, O'Reilly, four-six-four-oh. I have a 10-10S at 77th Avenue, between 164th and 166th. Building under construction. Request backup, and a bus, forthwith."

"Ten-Four, O'Reilly," Dispatch said. "Units inbound."

Erin put away her radio. Then she began climbing the ladder again.

"You don't want to go up there alone," Paulson warned. "He may have another gun."

"He's hurt," she replied. "I have to make sure he doesn't bleed out." The man above her was moaning quietly.

"For Christ's sake, let him," was Paulson's opinion. "He just tried to kill you. What if both of them are up there?"

"He's giving up," she retorted, still climbing. "He needs first aid. We're cops, Paulson. You're not in Baghdad anymore."

"Shit," Paulson muttered, feeding fresh shells into the breech of the shotgun. "You get killed; I'm not doing the paperwork."

"You're all heart," Erin said, reaching the top of the ladder. She thrust herself the rest of the way up, bringing the Glock in line.

A quick look told her there was no danger. A lone man in jeans and a dirty white T-shirt sat on the bare flakeboard, clutching one of his legs. Both lower limbs were peppered with buckshot. Blood was soaking his jeans.

"Come on up, Paulson!" she called down. "He's alone and he's hurt."

She recognized one of the four men from the heist, both from her own experience and from Cal's description. It was Mike, the weightlifter, the one with the shaved head and the crazy eyes. Those eyes didn't look so crazy now. He stared at Erin with a mix of terror, pain, and an odd, wrenching hope.

"Mike?"

"What?" He said, his voice tight with pain. "How'd you know my name? Shit, this hurts! I'm dying!"

"You're under arrest," she said, moving into the room. "For murder, armed robbery, attempted murder, and resisting arrest. But I'm going to take care of you. You're not going to die."

Paulson clambered up the ladder into the room. He regarded the wounded man dispassionately, the muzzle of the shotgun trained on Mike's head.

"Point that thing somewhere else," Erin said. She needed to administer first aid, and the last thing she wanted was a gun aimed anywhere close to her. She holstered her Glock and knelt beside Mike. The man was too frightened and hurt to even think of further resistance.

"Take off your shirt," she told him. "Wrap it around your left leg, where the bleeding is worst. Put pressure here, and hold it." Sirens were already loud and coming rapidly nearer. It must be the squad cars from the crime scene two blocks south.

The reinforcements were there quickly, four more cops spilling into the yard and securing the area. Then it was just a matter of waiting for the ambulance. A quick examination of Mike's wounds had told Erin they were painful, but not life-threatening. It was all meat and muscle damage, no punctured arteries. He'd recover, given time and decent medical care, both of which would be provided to him as a guest of the state of New York.

Chapter 12

Erin hadn't expected to be back at the hospital so soon. She, Rolf, and Paulson rode along in the ambulance. She had plenty of questions for Mike, but the paramedics had doped him up. He was so spaced out on painkillers, blood loss, and shock that he might as well be on the far side of the moon.

They pulled into the parking lot. The medics hopped out and deployed the stretcher. Erin stepped onto the back bumper of the ambulance and froze in surprise.

Camera flashbulbs went off like a firing squad. A dozen hands thrust microphones at her. Reporters shouted questions that blurred together into a chaotic wave of sound.

"No comment," she snapped, holding a hand in front of her eyes and wondering how the press had gotten word. Someone in the department must have leaked it, or someone with a police scanner had heard about the shootout and made a lucky guess. She took a firmer grip on Rolf's leash and followed the ambulance crew inside. Paulson, at her side, glared at the reporters and said nothing.

Inside, the medics wheeled the wounded man into surgery. Erin, Paulson, and two more cops took up positions guarding the room. She fingered the grip of her Glock and thought back over what had happened. Now that the danger was past, she felt suddenly shaky. If she hadn't jumped off the ladder when she did, she'd have taken a bullet. Her vest might have stopped it. Otherwise, she could've ended up like Brunanski. She shuddered, remembering how warm his blood had felt on her hands.

"O'Reilly! What the hell are you doing?"

Erin jumped. She spun and found herself face to face with Detective Spinelli. The little man had his hands on his hips, his thin mustache quivering with indignation. Just behind him, Detective Lyons stood with arms crossed, scowling.

"I'm guarding my prisoner," she said, hating the way her voice quivered. Erin berated herself for showing any weakness in front of these bastards.

"*Our* prisoner," Lyons growled.

"Screw you," Paulson snapped, taking a step forward. Spinelli reflexively backed away. "I tagged him, O'Reilly put the cuffs on. This is our collar."

"Yeah, good work, tough guy," Spinelli said, recovering himself. "You'll get a gold star on your fitness report. But we'll take over from here."

"The suspect's not in any condition to be questioned," Erin said. "He's under anesthetic and in surgery."

"Yeah, O'Reilly, I know," Spinelli said. "Whose fault is that? Now we've got to wait for hours to find out if he knows where the other one is, and those are hours we don't have. There's a cop killer still on the loose, and you've screwed up our best lead."

Sheer outrage rendered Erin incapable of speech for several seconds. Her hands clenched into fists. "You realize," she said at last, "that if we hadn't tracked him, there'd be two cop killers on the loose, not one. You didn't have a lead. If you hadn't rushed the takedown at the apartment—"

"That'll be enough, Officer," Spinelli interrupted. "I'll already be recommending a disciplinary board review your actions, and those of your trigger-happy partner here. I don't see any point in going over the same ground they'll be covering. I'm giving you an order. Go home. You are off this case."

"You can't order me to do Jack shit," Erin shot back. "I'm not in your chain of command."

"Okay, I'll get Murphy on the phone," Spinelli said. "He'll order you to do the same thing."

Murphy was on her side, but her Lieutenant wasn't about to pick an open fight with Homicide. Knowing she was beaten, Erin turned to Paulson. "Let's let the dicks watch Sleeping Beauty in there," she said. "We did the hard work, let them coast down Easy Street."

Paulson nodded. "Catch you later," he muttered and stalked away, his shotgun slanted over his shoulder. Erin didn't look back, not wanting to see the smug satisfaction on the detectives' faces. She and Rolf went out a side door to avoid the reporters clustered around the emergency room. They took a cab back to her car. Then, hands gripping her steering wheel in frustrated fury, she drove back to her apartment.

* * *

Erin didn't let her temper out until she was safely behind the closed door of her apartment. Then she slammed the heel of her hand against the wall and gave a cry of helpless rage. Rolf came up close beside her, tail wagging anxiously. She looked down at her partner and let some of the anger seep out of her. "It's all right, boy," she said. "I'm okay."

Rolf wasn't convinced. He flattened his ears back and thrust his muzzle against her hand. She stroked his head and sighed.

Maybe she should just walk away. The case was almost wrapped up anyway. Jake Gallagher was just a common street hood. Only dumb luck and quick motion had kept him out of police custody so far, and she couldn't imagine him staying ahead of the NYPD much longer. Find him and they'd find the painting. Then they'd lean on him to get the name of the buyer, and that would be the end of it.

"I'm not a detective," she said to Rolf, sinking onto the love seat opposite her TV. "I'm just a beat cop who was in the wrong place at the wrong time."

Rolf didn't disagree. He liked it when Erin talked to him, so he encouraged her as well as he could, staring intently into her eyes and cocking his head, making her the center of his attention.

Her phone rang, startling her out of her self-pity. It was an unknown number, with a New York area code. She considered letting it go unanswered, but her dad had driven that lesson into her early.

"A police officer never lets it ring, kiddo," he'd said. *"You're always on duty, even when you're not."*

She swiped the screen. "O'Reilly," she said.

"Ah, my dear girl!" a man exclaimed.

The round, rolling tone was unmistakable. "Dr. Van Ormond," she said.

"Please, call me Van. As I told you at our first meeting, I wish to count you as a friend. And how are you, my dear?"

"I'm fine," Erin said. "How'd you get this number?"

"I prevailed upon our mutual acquaintance to provide me with the means of contacting you," he said. "Dear girl, please accept my condolences. Such a terrible, terrible business."

"Yeah, it was," she said. "Dr. Van Ormond, is there something I can help you with? I've had a long couple of days and—"

"Of course, of course," the Englishman said. "I shan't keep you long. I merely wished to commiserate with you on the subject of the late unfortunate events, and to inquire as to the status of your investigation."

Erin blinked. "Doctor, I don't know what the rules are in England, but over here, we're not allowed to talk about details of an ongoing investigation."

"Oh, I say," Van Ormond exclaimed. "I shouldn't dream of placing you in any sort of false position. I suppose you are not close to the heart of the investigation in any case."

"What do you mean?" Erin asked sharply. She was still feeling raw from the tongue-lashing Lyons and Spinelli had given her.

"Only that you are an ordinary patrol officer, my dear," he said, and though his voice was still cheerful, there was a hint of condescension in it that raised her hackles. "A bobby, we call them. I shouldn't think they would trouble you with the tedious details of such an investigation. Back onto the street with you, dear girl. The thrill of the hunt, tally-ho and all that. You must find the very idea of detective work a dreadful bore. All that sitting behind desks, filling out papers."

"We do a lot of paperwork in Patrol Division, too," she said, becoming increasingly annoyed. She wished she hadn't taken her dad's advice. "Look, Doctor, I really can't help you right now."

"Indeed not, poor girl," he said. "Alas, I fear the glory of re-covering the Madonna may go to some other bold investigator."

Erin saw Spinelli in her mind's eye, the little man with his ridiculous scrawny mustache, preening at a press conference he'd called in his own honor. Her jaw tightened. "No one's recovered the Madonna yet," she snapped. "For all I know, it's out of the country, or at the bottom of the East River. And for all I care, it can stay there. You think this is about glory? One of ours got killed, Doctor. I was there, and I got his blood all over me, and that's what this is about. It doesn't matter if the bastard who did it runs to the other side of the goddamn world; I'll find him there. We're close."

She ran out of breath and paused to let her lungs catch up. Rolf was on his feet, sensing her agitation, awaiting instruction.

"I seem to have hurt your feelings," Van Ormond said in a much softer tone. "I'm terribly sorry, my dear girl."

"Officer," she said through gritted teeth.

"I beg your pardon?"

"It's Officer O'Reilly. I've been wearing a shield for eleven years," Erin said, speaking slowly and distinctly. "I'm not your girl, dear or not."

"Ah," he said. "Well, I'm terribly sorry if I have offended you. I certainly intended no such thing. I shall leave you to your duties and your ruminations. Again, please accept my condolences on the passing of dear Officer Bukowski."

Erin put a hand over her face and rubbed her eyes. "Brunanski," she growled. "John Brunanski. You could at least get his name right."

"Yes, of course," Van Ormond said. "Brunanski."

"Goodbye, Doctor," Erin said firmly.

"Good day, Officer—" he began, but she hung up on him mid-sentence.

The buzz on her apartment intercom followed so quickly that she hadn't even put her phone down. She punched the button on the box. "What?" she snapped, much more sharply than she'd intended.

"It's Luke," the answer came, sounding cautious. "I've got a guy here who wants to talk to you."

"What guy? What do you want?" she demanded. She wasn't happy about him giving her phone number to Van Ormond.

There was a short pause. Then another voice, heavily accented, spoke. "*Fräulein* O'Reilly?"

"Dr. Schenk," Erin said in surprise.

"*Ja*. May I speak with you?"

"Okay, sure," she said, for lack of a better idea, and buzzed them in. She had a few moments before they arrived, and used them to straighten up the apartment as best she could. Fortunately, she'd always been fairly neat, and didn't have much stuff to begin with, but she wasn't used to visitors. A few clothes were lying out and some books were strewn on the coffee table.

She was still arranging the books on her shelf when her guests knocked on the door. She ran a hand through her hair, looked down at herself, realized she was still wearing her uniform, and decided she didn't care. She opened the door.

Luke smiled at her, but his glance was wary as he took in the lingering irritation in her face. Rudolf Schenk seemed not to notice. The gaunt German stalked into her apartment and cast a contemptuous glance around the place. Erin winced inwardly. She favored black-and-white photos of New York cityscapes, and she could imagine what this student of the Renaissance must think of her choice of décor.

Rolf checked out the visitors. He recognized Luke with a brisk wag of his tail, but gave Schenk a long, careful look.

"A very fine *Hund*, Officer O'Reilly," Schenk said. "He is German, *ja*?"

"From Bavaria," Erin said. "The NYPD gets most of its dogs from German breeders. He was trained in your native language, Doctor."

"*Sehr gut*," Schenk said, nodding. Rolf, having decided the man posed no threat, retreated to Erin's side.

"Can I get you anything?" she asked awkwardly. "I've got Guinness in the fridge."

"That would be great," Luke said. "Thanks."

"*Ja*, thank you," Schenk said. He folded his long, spindly limbs down onto the love seat, clasped his hands above his knees, and leaned forward. Erin thought of old men she'd seen sitting on park benches. They always looked a little lost, like they were waiting for something that would never come. Luke sat beside the professor.

Erin fetched three bottles from the refrigerator, filled the glasses, and brought the drinks to the coffee table. She pulled a straight-backed chair from her little dining table into the living room and took a seat.

"Okay, what's up?" she asked.

"I have spoken with *Herr* Devins regarding the Madonna," Schenk said. "I know you are seeking her. This is a matter in which I have some... small interest."

"Yes, I know," she said, recalling what Luke had told her about the professor. "You're an expert in lost Nazi treasure."

"That is true," Schenk said. "But this is *ein bisschen anders*. This painting has personal significance."

Erin, thinking back to the art gallery, recalled how Schenk had recognized the marks on the Raphael as bloodstains. A sudden thought struck her with the force of a fist to the stomach. "Did you already know about her? Before she was found?"

Schenk stared at her with his haunted, burning eyes. "*Ja, Fräulein*. My mother told me of her."

Erin and Luke both leaned forward as the professor began to explain.

Chapter 13

"The brother of my mother was a dealer in rare antiquities. His name was Julius Mandelbaum. This name, it means nothing to you, but if you were a dealer in paintings, in the time between the wars, you would have heard it often. He was very well-to-do, very wealthy.

"Many sellers of artworks are unable to part with their greatest treasures. As with them, so with *mein Onkel*. His home, in Vienna, was a palace of wonders. Often, when I was a young boy, my mother told me of this house. It was filled with paintings, statues, shelves of rare books.

"His greatest treasure was a little painting, which he kept in a cabinet beside his bed. She came to him by a long and difficult road, from a dealer in Sienna who purchased her from a Florentine nobleman who... it is no matter. It is enough that she was thought to be a Raphael. *Herr* Mandelbaum never authenticated her, for he had no thought to sell her. He did not even show her to his guests. Only his close family knew of her.

"My parents lived in Berlin when the Nazis came to power in 1933. *Mein Vater* always called Hitler 'That second-rate painter.' Hitler had aspirations of painting, did you know? But his works were derivative, puerile.

"I will quickly gloss over the whole history of those years, how everything was taken from my family, as from so many others. Jews were forbidden to hold government positions. Then we could not serve in the military, though in the Great War more Jews, in proportion, fought for Germany than did any other group or sect. Then we could not marry non-Jews, and so on, and on.

"My father was a wise man, and he took thought for the future. Before Jewish moneys were frozen, he took from the bank all his savings and used them to purchase gold and diamonds, small and portable valuables. These he hid in several places. He began to seek ways to escape, though he thought himself a German and the land had ever been his home.

"It was not so easy as it seems. Other countries were not so willing to welcome refugee Jews. You must remember, *Fräulein*, it was the Great Depression. You think a country like America, with unemployment then of one in four, would open her doors to immigrants? You see how it is even today with your Mexicans? And my parents knew nothing, how could they know, of what was to come. Julius Mandelbaum was not afraid. After all, he was not even in Germany. But in 1938 came the *Anschluss*, when Austria was taken by Hitler. Hitler was Austrian himself, did you know?

"Then came the *Kristallnacht*. You have heard of this, *ja*?"

Erin shook her head. She'd found world history one of the most boring subjects in high school, and what she'd learned had wandered out of her head at the end of her last semester.

Schenk rubbed his bony hands together, as if they were cold. "The pretext was the murder of the German ambassador to Poland, by a Jewish boy. But this was only the excuse, a way for the Nazis to see how far they might go, what the German people would accept. The ambassador was shot on the seventh of November, 1938, and died two days later. The *Kristallnacht* was the night following his death. So you see, it was all planned by the Nazis ahead of time, else how could so large a *pogrom* occur on such short notice?

"It was humiliation, vandalism, murder. All of it planned by Hitler's stormtroopers, across Germany and Austria, but in Vienna it was worst. The synagogues were burned and broken, Jewish businesses and homes looted.

"*Mein Onkel's* home was no refuge. The mob came, shattered the windows. Julius ran upstairs, to his bedroom, to save his most precious treasure. His wife, *Tante* Rachel, was there, with his two daughters, hiding beneath the bed. Julius went to the cabinet and unlocked it with the key he wore always about his neck. Even as he reached in to take the Madonna, a brownshirt, one of the Nazi barbarians, fired from the doorway with a revolver. You were correct, *Fräulein*. The bullet almost struck the Madonna. His blood spattered her breast. He fell before the painting and died there, before the eyes of his wife and children. Rachel held her hands over her daughters' mouths so they would not scream. She still bore the marks of my cousins' teeth upon her palms three days later, when she told the story to my mother.

"The brownshirt cared nothing for the art of a great master, but he knew Julius had treasured the Madonna, so he thought her of some value. He took her from the cabinet and she disappeared into the charnel-house of the *Shoah*."

"The Holocaust," Luke translated.

"*Ja*," Schenk said. "Rachel and my cousins remained hidden until the smoke drove them out. The mob had set a fire, and they were scorched and choked when they ran from the house. All the rest of the treasures, which Julius Mandelbaum had gathered all his life, went up in smoke, as did Julius himself. And that was the end of the palace of my dreams."

"Jesus," Erin said quietly.

Schenk's eyes held hers with their dark, haunted intensity. "*Nein, Fräulein.* Quite the opposite."

"So you knew the Madonna was real, before you saw her," she said, forcing herself to think like a twenty-first century cop.

"Not quite," Schenk said. "I knew she was the same painting that in *mein Onkel's* collection held place of honor. He thought her genuine, but I could not know until I saw her myself, and heard the counsel of experts."

"Like Luke," she said.

"Like me," Luke said agreeably.

"So she really belongs to your aunt Rachel," Erin said. Seeing the slight shake of Schenk's head, she tried again. "Or your cousins?"

"*Nein, Fräulein.* They came north, to Berlin, to seek aid from my parents. But things grew worse, and the war came. My family went into hiding, but there was not space enough for all together. My parents had a friend, a Christian priest, who was opposed to the Nazis. He hid them. *Mein Vater* found a place for Rachel and her children with another foe of the regime, but they were betrayed and arrested. All of them together, the Jews, the good man who helped them, and his family, finished in the camps. Like Julius, they turned to ash."

"And the rest of your family?" Erin asked in a small, hesitant voice.

"I am the only one left," Schenk said.

Erin sat quietly for a moment, thinking. Under the weight of such a historic tragedy, the fate of a painting, no matter how valuable, was almost trivial. But people had died for the Madonna, both in 1938 and seventy-five years later. She couldn't bring Julius Mandelbaum's murderer to justice. His killer was an anonymous Nazi thug, probably dead for half a century. But his modern-day counterparts had killed a New York police officer, and that made them her business.

She looked at the professor. "Why are you telling me this, Dr. Schenk?"

"You seek the Madonna, *Fräulein*," he replied. "I wish to help you. But you do not trust easily. Tell me, Officer O'Reilly. If you learned my story from another man, what would you think?"

"I'd think you had an excellent motive to steal your old family treasure," she said, meeting his straight talk with her own. "You'd be my number-one suspect."

"Exactly," Schenk said, pointing a long finger at her. "So it is better you hear it from my mouth, so you know I have nothing to hide."

Erin wondered about that. She knew, from her years pounding the pavement, that most criminals were basically idiots. Many were hooked on drugs, drunk, or otherwise impaired. Outthinking them was pretty easy. But the trouble with dealing with clever criminals was that they knew how to act innocent. How could she know the difference between an intelligent crook and an innocent man? Schenk was plenty smart, but was he telling the truth, or throwing her off his trail?

If he was blowing smoke, it meant Luke was probably in on it, too, she thought with a sudden shudder of paranoia. Otherwise Schenk wouldn't be here. He'd be down at the station, talking to Lyons and Spinelli.

She looked at Luke and saw him watching her with nothing but concern in his eyes. No, she couldn't believe he was in with the thieves. It was too crazy. He'd brought her there on a date—brought a cop to a crime about to happen! But then, what better alibi than to have a police officer on his arm all evening?

Erin's thoughts were tying themselves up in knots. She shook her head to clear it.

"Erin? Are you okay?" Luke asked, leaning forward.

"Yeah, I'm fine," she said. "Dr. Schenk?"

"*Ja?*" The professor stared intently at her.

"You know a lot about art, right?"

"It is my life," he said, with no hint of hyperbole.

"Who do you think would pay to steal this painting?"

Schenk tapped a bony finger against his lips. "Other than the obvious, you mean?"

"Obvious?" Erin echoed.

"Phineas Van Ormond, of course," Schenk said.

Chapter 14

"No," Luke said. "Absolutely not."

"Wait a minute," Erin said, holding up a hand. "Professor, why do you say that?"

Schenk looked like he was scowling, but it might have just been his normal facial expression. "He believes he has the right to possess works of art," Schenk said. "He thinks that merely because he knows much on a subject, he is more deserving of such a possession."

Erin cleared her throat. "Professor, that's not really a very compelling motive. You could say the same thing about any number of people at the gala. I mean, I know the painting's worth a lot of money. Do you think he's planning to sell the Madonna, or—"

"*Nein!*" Schenk snapped, making an explosive gesture with his hands. "What does it matter, what he does with her? Whether he keeps her as a prisoner, or sells her as a slave, it makes no difference."

Erin sighed and ran a hand through her hair. "Professor, there must be dozens of guys like him in the art world."

"There aren't many like Van," Luke said. "He's brilliant, Erin. And I'm sorry, *Herr Doktor*, but you've got him wrong. He's not a killer, and he's not the sort of guy who'd hire thugs to steal a painting. He'd be too afraid the work would be damaged or lost." The art appraiser shook his head. "I don't believe it."

Schenk abruptly stood. "I have wasted your time, *Herr* Devins, *Fräulein* O'Reilly. I apologize. I thought you wished to solve this mystery. Good day." He began to walk toward the door.

"Hold it," Erin said sharply. "I'm not an art expert. I don't tell you what to say in your lectures. You're not a cop. You don't get to decide who to arrest."

Schenk paused, his hand on the doorknob. Turning, he made eye contact with Erin. To her surprise, a smile spread across his gaunt and hollow face, slow and faint, but genuine. "I think, *Fräulein*, that your anger is both your weakness and your strength. I think you will not rest until you have found your thief. Good luck to you."

Then he was gone, the door swinging shut behind him. Erin, torn between bewilderment and irritation, clenched her fists and blew out a lungful of air through gritted teeth.

"Erin?" Luke said hesitantly. "I'm sorry. I thought we might be able to help. I was trying—"

"Yeah, I know," she said, loosening her fingers. "It's okay. It was a good thought, bringing him here."

"You still thinking about Van?" Luke asked.

"Yeah," she said. "He called me, you know. On my cell. Which I didn't give him."

"Ah," Luke said uncomfortably. "Right. Did he bother you? He wanted to pass on his condolences, on account of what happened."

"He was kind of an ass," she said.

"Really?" Luke said. "That's hard to believe. He's a nice guy, Erin. Honest. He's just upset about this whole thing. Everyone is. All the dealers and historians who were there—"

"Brunanski got killed!" Erin snapped. She took a deep breath, reminding herself that Luke wasn't a police officer, hadn't known Brunanski. "I've seen people die before, Luke. You work Patrol, you get called to accidents, shootings, domestics that go bad. But I never had an officer go down on my watch."

"Erin, you weren't even on duty," Luke said quietly. "It wasn't your fault."

"Of course it was!" she retorted. "I saw it, I knew what was happening. I should've had my gun with me. They never should've made it outside."

"Christ, Erin, there were four of them, all armed," Luke said. "They'd have killed you, too."

Some of the anger seeped out of Erin. "Yeah, I know," she sighed. "I'm just sick of people talking like the painting's the only thing that matters. Anyone wearing a shield, they're not after an art thief right now; they're chasing cop-killers."

"Right, I get that," Luke said. He put a gentle hand on her arm. "Just remember, I don't always see things the way an officer does. I'm new at this whole police thing."

"Van Ormond's still gotta be a suspect," she said. "Doesn't mean I think he did it. Means he might've."

It was Luke's turn to sigh. "You do what you have to do," he said. "Believe it or not, I do want to help."

"Do you have that list I asked for?" Erin asked, taking the opportunity to change the subject. "The guys you think might do this sort of thing?"

"Uh huh," Luke said, drawing a folded piece of paper out of the inside pocket of his sport coat and laying it on the coffee table. "But Erin, I've got to ask you. How far do you intend to go with this? Some of these people are powerful, with connections."

"All the way," she said without flinching. "Jake Gallagher and his dirtbag friends killed a cop. John Brunanski was one of ours, and I promised him I'd get them. Those assholes Lyons and Spinelli may have tried to kick me off the case, but they can't stop me. As long as I don't work on the clock, and don't involve other officers, they can't do a damn thing to me." This wasn't quite true, but Erin didn't particularly care.

"So what are you going to do?" he asked.

"First, I'm going to read your list of names. You're going to tell me why each of them is on the list. And then I'm going to find out who was behind this mess and take him down."

"Can we crack open a bottle of wine while we talk?" Luke suggested.

Erin couldn't help a small smile. "Are you trying to turn a criminal investigation into a date?"

He shrugged. "Sitting together and talking, sharing an activity, cooperating... sounds like a date to me. Anyway, you're not on the clock. You said so yourself."

"We don't give out many kisses in the interrogation room," she said. Her anger was gone now.

Luke grinned. "Then it's a good thing we're not at your precinct."

She snatched the folded note off the table. "Do you want to flirt, or do you want to catch the bad guys?"

"I never claimed to be good at catching bad guys," he said.

*   *   *

An hour and most of a bottle of wine later, Erin was ready to burn down the Metropolitan Museum of Art, on the condition that she could stuff it full of collectors and critics first. It wasn't a lack of suspects that was bothering her, but the opposite. Luke had been as good as his word, giving her five names of art dealers who were known, or suspected, of dealing under the table, but he freely admitted there were probably ten times that many in Manhattan alone.

"Let's recap," she said, looking down at her notepad, which was now full of scribbled information. "We've got five names: Philippe Clemenceau, Roy Atkins, Dominique de Vere, Omar Haddad, and Adlai Martin. Clemenceau likes Renaissance painters and is known to trade on the black market in Europe. Atkins is a wealthy playboy who thinks money lets him ignore the rules. De Vere is suspected of murdering her husband three years ago on Corsica and was arrested, but not convicted. Haddad comes from oil money, which isn't a crime, but smuggled marble statues out of Italy, which is. If we want him, we'll have to get in line behind the Italians, who are currently trying to extradite him. Then there's Martin, who's probably a sociopath and whose wife divorced him and is suing him for alimony and domestic abuse allegations. Did I miss anything?" She threw her arms up. "Luke, what the hell is the matter with these people? This is art. Paintings, beautiful things. Why is the market full of scumbags?"

Luke smiled sadly. "Beautiful, *expensive* paintings, Erin. The only people who can afford to buy works like the Madonna are people who have an absurd amount of personal wealth. Unfortunately, that's not exactly a random cross-section of society. Psychopaths congregate at the high end of the economic spectrum."

"So how do we narrow this down?" Erin asked. "They're all guilty of *something*."

"Like I keep saying, I'm not a cop," Luke said.

"Okay," she said, "We look for means, motive, and opportunity. All of them have motive. This painting is priceless, and they're all art collectors and dealers. So we need to think of the other criteria."

"All of them have means, too," he said. "They're all millionaires."

"True, but they need contacts," Erin said. "You can't just throw money at something like this. The perp needed to get in touch with our local boys. It's not exactly the sort of circle these high-rollers usually move in. We need a suspect who'd be willing to hire muscle, but wouldn't already have any of their own."

Luke snapped his fingers. "Right. If they have their own crew, they wouldn't need to hire these amateurs."

"Okay," Erin said. "Did this de Vere chick kill her husband herself, or did she hire it out?"

"She wasn't convicted," he dryly reminded her. "But the accusation was that she stabbed him through the throat with a toasting fork. She claimed it was housebreakers. The jury let her go, but only because the prosecution botched the case."

"So she's someone who takes care of her own problems," Erin said. "But on the other hand, that means she doesn't have a hit man on retainer. Do you know if this crew is all in town?"

"Yeah, they're all in New York," Luke said. "Four of them were at the gala."

"They were?" Erin exclaimed.

"Of course. It was the major art event of the season. I'm only surprised Haddad didn't show."

"Was he supposed to?"

"I have a copy of the guest list," Luke said. "I saw his name on it, but he wasn't there."

A thrill ran through Erin. "I need to talk to him, find out why he was a no-show."

Luke produced his smartphone and brought up an address. "Here's the house Haddad is renting," he said, showing it to her.

"If you could, though, please don't mention that I told you. I move in these circles a lot, and if word gets around that I'm handing out tips to law enforcement, people won't talk to me."

"Criminals won't talk to you, you mean," she corrected.

"There's a lot of gray areas in the art world," he said. "Sometimes it's genuinely hard to know if something was legally obtained. And these are people who like their privacy. Nobody likes a cop nosing into their private affairs."

"Sure thing, Luke," Erin said. "I'll keep your name out of it. And thank you, for everything. You've been a big help."

"Just trying to impress a girl," he said with a grin.

Erin felt excited, her nerves tingling. Some of it was the wine, some of it the new lead. And some, she admitted, was Luke Devins. She leaned toward him. "Well, maybe I'm impressed," she said quietly. "Are you sure you don't want a cop involved in your private affairs?"

Their eyes met. "How involved do you want to be?"

"Thoroughly." She slipped her hand around the back of his neck and drew him into a kiss.

Luke might not be great at catching bad guys, but Erin found he made up for it with other talents.

* * *

"You talking to Haddad?" Luke asked an hour later.

Erin glanced over her shoulder at him as she buttoned her blouse. "Him first," she said. "Then the others."

Luke smiled. "Go get 'em," he said. "Call me after, though. Let me know how it went?"

"Will do," she said. She wasn't wearing her uniform, since technically she wasn't on duty. But she buckled her Glock onto her belt and clipped on her shield.

Luke had gotten out of bed and was quickly dressing. "You really think you'll need the gun?"

"If he's the guy, then Jake Gallagher may be there," she said. "Anyway, you know where I am. Just in case anything happens."

"Shouldn't you have backup?" he asked. "If this is dangerous..."

"I can't call for backup," Erin said. "Not unless I see a crime actually being committed. Everything I'm doing is unofficial, thanks to those two jackasses from Homicide. Besides, I'll have Rolf."

"Won't it spook him, having the dog there?"

"I hope it does," Erin said. "I want him off-balance."

Chapter 15

From Luke's description of a wealthy playboy art collector, Erin was expecting Omar Haddad's house to be something ridiculous. A gated mansion, maybe, with a swimming pool, tennis courts, and a sculpture garden. The address was in Forest Hills, southwest of the Museum. It was a nice part of town, but hardly the sort of place for an oil baron.

She drove along tree-lined avenues, past pleasant red-brick houses and apartments. The early-evening sun slanted through the leaves of the trees. The house that matched the address Luke had given her looked no different from those on either side, very middle-class and ordinary. She double-checked the number, then got out of the squad car and, Rolf's leash in hand, approached the building.

The doorbell was answered by a tall man with a black goatee, skin the color of old leather, and the stern, polite manner of a trained butler.

"Good afternoon, madam," he said with a distinct British accent. "How may I assist you?"

"Sir, my name is Erin O'Reilly," she said. "I'm an officer with the New York Police Department. I'd like to speak with Omar Haddad."

"Master Haddad is within," the man said. "But he is indisposed, and I fear he is not receiving visitors today."

"Sir, this is not a social call," Erin said. "I'm investigating a serious crime, and I believe he has information which may help resolve it."

"Madam," the man said severely, "Master Haddad has done nothing illegal. He is convalescing from an unfortunate accident, and will be entirely unable to assist you in your inquiries."

Erin fought her impatience. "Sir, with respect, I'd like to be the judge of that. Please ask him if he would be willing to speak with me. It's about the theft of the Raphael Madonna from the art museum. I think he'll find it's in his best interest to talk to me."

The butler considered her. "Very well, madam," he said. "Please be patient."

The door closed in her face. It wasn't quite a slam, but it was a very solid and definite closure. Erin sighed. Rolf, recognizing that nothing was happening at the moment, sat on the front steps and stared at his surroundings.

It was only a few minutes until the door opened again. The butler, his face showing a hint of irritation, stood to one side. "Please come in, madam," he said. As she started forward, he added, "But your pet must remain outside."

"He's not my pet," Erin retorted. "He's my partner. He's a trained K-9 of the NYPD. He won't chew on anything I don't tell him to. But he goes where I go."

"A dog, madam?" he said, in the same tone he might have used if Erin had suggested dragging in a dead rat. "That filthy creature does not pass this threshold."

"Okay," Erin said. "Then you can go back and tell your boss that thanks to your lack of hospitality, his guest has gone away. Then you can deal with the detectives who'll be coming by later. They may not be so polite." She turned away.

"Madam," the butler said, before she'd taken more than a step. She paused and half-turned. "The brute may enter," he said reluctantly. "But you will be held responsible for whatever it does."

"I always am," she shot back as she strode in. Rolf marched beside her, ears at attention, tail swinging from side to side. Erin could have sworn the dog looked smug.

The house was obviously rented out, fully furnished. The style was modern American, without particularly fancy decoration. This was not what she had expected at all.

Nor was the man she found reclining on the couch. Omar Haddad was younger than she was, not more than twenty-seven or twenty-eight. He was very good-looking, almost movie-star handsome. His features were smooth and regular, his skin tone a warm caramel. He was clean-shaven and his eyes... there was no other way to describe them. They smoldered. He was wearing a silk dressing gown. A silver tray lay on the coffee table with a teapot, a cup of steaming tea, and several newspapers.

"Officer Erin O'Reilly, sir," the butler said. He bowed and stepped back into the doorway, from which he stared balefully at Rolf.

"Thank you, Ibrahim," the young man said. His voice was soft, almost melodious. He seemed mildly surprised at Erin's appearance, his eyes traveling over her with more than casual attention. She realized he hadn't known she was a woman ahead of time. "Officer O'Reilly, I am Omar Haddad. I would stand to welcome you, but I fear my leg is injured. Come, share a cup of tea with me."

"That's all right, Mr. Haddad," she said. "I don't need anything. I just wanted to ask you a few questions."

"Please, I insist," he said. "For my sake."

"Okay, thanks," Erin said, not knowing what else to say. She preferred coffee or alcohol to tea, but she figured she'd better be polite.

"Ibrahim, another cup for my guest," Haddad said. The tall man, still glowering, bowed again and departed, returning with a teacup and saucer. "That will be all, Ibrahim," the art dealer said. The servant frowned, but he left the room.

"Now then," Haddad said, when Erin had taken a seat in the chair to his right and he had poured her a cup of tea. "How may I be of assistance?"

"Mr. Haddad, yesterday the Queens Museum of Art was robbed," she began. "A painting believed to be a Raphael was stolen by armed men dressed as security guards. A police officer was killed trying to stop them."

"I am aware of all this," he said, gesturing to the newspapers on the table.

Erin looked straight at him. "Mr. Haddad, you were on the guest list for the gala at the Museum. Why didn't you attend?"

"A moderate inconvenience prevented me," he said, gesturing to his leg. "I was interested in acquiring a young stallion from a farm near Albany, and had flown there for the day. Unfortunately, the stallion was rather spirited, and I was thrown. The physician says my leg is not broken, but my knee was dislocated."

"Can anyone verify your whereabouts?" she asked.

"I traveled in a small airplane," he said. "The pilot can confirm this, as can the proprietor of the stable, several stablehands, and my manservant." He paused and regarded Erin. His eyes slowly took on a coldness that startled her. She'd seen eyes like those on hardened street criminals. They were a killer's eyes. "Officer, you surely are not suggesting that I had anything to do with the unfortunate events of last night?"

"Did you want the Madonna?" Erin countered. When doing interrogations, she'd found that answering the subject's questions shifted control of the conversation. It was better to keep them responding, and to simply ignore any questions that came back her way.

"Of course I want it," Haddad said. "Have you seen it? It is a true masterpiece. Any man who appreciates true art would desire such a treasure."

"What were you prepared to pay for the painting?" she asked, refusing to be put on the defensive.

"For an original, undiscovered Raphael?" Haddad smiled, and a little warmth returned to his eyes. "Officer, the whole point of an auction is that no one knows how much the other bidders are prepared to offer. Otherwise, we might as well simply slap a price tag on the painting and put it in a shop window, like those dreadful paintings by that American who paints country cottages with windows all aglow."

"You're a dealer in rare art and antiques," Erin said. "What are you doing in Queens, in this house?" She waved a hand at the very ordinary, very American décor.

"I am fond of the trees."

"The trees?" Erin blinked.

"My homeland is Saudi Arabia," Haddad said. "It is a desert nation. Oh, there are trees in Riyadh, but they are sparse and skeletal compared to these lush, lovely trees which grow in your marvelous climate. So whenever I come to your country, or any similar place, I rent a house with a yard. It must have trees and long, green grass."

"I see," she said. "Sir, you did come here to view the Raphael, with an eye to buying it, didn't you?"

"I did," he agreed. "I am as irritated as you that someone has stolen it. I do hope you find them."

Erin cursed inwardly. He was giving nothing away. If he was guilty, he was doing an excellent job of hiding it. "Have you seen the Madonna, Mr. Haddad?"

"Not in person," he said. "I intended to visit the Museum today, or perhaps early next week. Now, of course, that serves little purpose. I would very much like to see it, however. If your department recovers the painting, I trust it will be placed back on display. Is it true that the blood of its previous owner, the Jew, is spattered on it? I have heard as much."

She stared at him, remembering Schenk's story of his uncle's murder. "Tell me, Mr. Haddad," she said, unable to help herself. "Would having Jewish blood on a painting make it worth less to you, or more?"

Haddad smiled again. Erin still thought he was handsome, but she was liking his face less and less with every moment of the conversation. "It serves as a badge of authenticity," he said. "Though I do wish the man who owned the painting had possessed the decency to die somewhere else, leaving the painting unspoilt. That sort of blood does tend to contaminate that which it touches."

"Sir," Erin said with slow, careful self-control, "do you know anything at all that could help our investigation into this robbery?"

"I know that there have been several interested parties, each looking into acquiring the painting," he said. "I have my agents, as do they. We all keep an eye on one another, you see."

"And?" she prompted.

"Roy Atkins and Adlai Martin are two names which were brought to my attention as competitors," he said. "They have each purchased tickets to the auction to be held at the conclusion of the tour."

Erin nodded. Haddad had actually told her something useful there. These men were either extremely clever, or innocent. "What about Professor Schenk?"

"The German Jew?" Haddad snorted. "He could never afford such a painting. He has no money to speak of. His interest is solely intellectual and sentimental."

"Phineas Van Ormond?" Erin tried.

"Another academic," he said with a dismissive wave of his hand. "He never even engaged a professional to make an appraisal."

"I just have one more question, Mr. Haddad," she said. "Is this the sort of painting that can be sold on the black market?"

"No, Officer," Haddad said quietly. "This painting is too unique. Those who stole the painting will deliver it to their employer. Then it will disappear into his private collection. It is a pity. I would like to own it. How is your tea?"

"Fine," Erin said, looking down at her cup. She hadn't taken even a sip.

"I am pleased to hear it. Is there anything else I can do to aid you?"

"If you think of anything, please let me know," Erin said, standing up. She laid one of her cards on the table. "Thank you for the tea."

"Officer," he said. "Where I come from, we still cut off the hands of thieves. If you do find these men, do not be gentle with them."

"I'll keep that in mind," Erin said. Ibrahim had returned, by some sort of servant telepathy, and once more filled the doorway. The tall Arab led her and Rolf back out of the house and into the quiet evening air.

Chapter 16

Erin sank behind the wheel of her car. She sat there for a moment, thinking. Then she shook her head and sighed. The sun had gone down on the longest day she could remember. She didn't even have the energy to be angry anymore.

But she couldn't sit there all night. There was still work to do. She started the car and pulled out her phone, calling Luke.

"Is everything okay?" he asked immediately.

"Yeah, I'm fine," she said, thinking, *civilians*. "But it's a washout. He's sleazy, sure, but he's got an alibi that looks like it'll hold up."

"Okay," Luke said. "So what now?"

"Now I run down the other leads," Erin replied. "Once I've talked to all the folks on your list, I'll go home and grab some sleep. Maybe things will look different in the morning."

"Do you want anything..." he began, then backtracked. "I mean, is there anything else I can..."

She had to smile. "I know what you mean, Luke, and you're sweet. You get some rest. I'll call you."

"All right. Erin?"

"Yeah?"

"Thank you."

"Thank you. Good night, Luke."

*   *   *

Erin had four more names to run down. Philippe Clemen-ceau and Adlai Martin were in their Manhattan apartments. Roy Atkins and Dominique de Vere, by sheer good luck, were both staying at the same hotel, the Hilton at JFK Airport. She owed Luke big for the tips he'd given her. Without his insider knowledge, she'd have been shooting in the dark.

It was getting late, and there was no guarantee any of her targets would be in. She had phone numbers, but the element of surprise was valuable, and calling ahead would tip them off. On the other hand, driving around New York City on a wild-goose chase wasn't her idea of a fun evening.

She compromised and called the Manhattan guys, figuring she could drive to the Hilton in Queens without wasting too much time. Martin was first on her list. She dialed his number from her car.

"Hello?"

The voice on the phone was wary. Erin wished she could see his face.

"Mr. Martin?"

"Who is this?"

"Sir, I'm Officer O'Reilly, with the NYPD, and—"

"Listen," he snapped, cutting her off. "Whatever that bitch told you, I never laid a hand on her. You got that?"

She remembered Luke had told her that Martin was going through a messy divorce, with allegations of abuse. "Sir, I'm not calling regarding that particular matter. I just wanted to ask you a few questions about—"

"Call Rinkmeyer, Spencer, and Flynn," Martin interrupted again. "They'll answer your goddamn questions." Then he hung up.

Erin sighed. Martin's lawyers were probably closed for the night, and it'd be useless to call them anyway. Her gut told her Martin was innocent. Well, not completely. He was probably guilty of whatever his soon-to-be-ex-wife said he was. But he'd assumed a call from the police was related to his divorce proceedings. It would've taken a hell of an actor to play things so believably without advance notice.

She'd loop back to him later, if necessary. For now, she had three names left on her list. She called Clemenceau next.

"Good evening." This voice was smooth, cultured, with just a faint hint of a French accent.

"Good evening, sir. Mr. Clemenceau?"

"Indeed I am. To whom am I speaking?"

"Sir, I'm Officer Erin O'Reilly, with the NYPD. I hope this isn't an inconvenient time."

"Not at all, Officer. How may I be of assistance?" He was pretty much the opposite of Martin, all suave manners. If he was startled at being contacted by the police, he wasn't giving any hint of it.

"I'd like to speak with you about the Orphans of Europe art exhibit," she said.

"Pursuant to your investigation into the theft of its centerpiece, of course," Clemenceau said. "I doubt if I can shed significant light upon the subject, but I would be delighted to speak with you, Officer."

"Could I talk to you this evening, in person?"

"Madam," he said, "I am entirely at your disposal. Do you have my address?"

"I do."

"I shall inform the footman in my building of your impending arrival. Simply furnish him with your name, and he shall direct you to my chambers."

Erin almost snorted at the last word. His *chambers?* Who the hell was this guy? "Thank you, sir," was what she said out loud. "I have to make the drive from Queens. I'll be there in a half hour or so."

"I eagerly await your arrival."

* * *

Erin brought Rolf with her. The dog was partly for moral support, partly to see if she could shake up the smooth customer. Clemenceau's address was in Midtown Manhattan, one of the most expensive neighborhoods in one of the most expensive cities on Earth. She didn't even want to guess at his monthly rent.

His apartment was on the twenty-fifth floor of a high-rise. She took advantage of a reserved police parking space, took a moment to rub some of the drowse out of her eyes, and got Rolf out of the back of the Charger. The footman was expecting her, just as Clemenceau had said. He showed her to the bank of elevators, and even insisted on pressing the button for the proper floor. She spent the ride up wondering whether the gold plating on the elevator walls was genuine. She scratched at it with a fingernail and decided it was.

She rang his doorbell at nine thirty on the dot. A few seconds later, the door opened.

"Officer, please come in," Philippe Clemenceau said.

Erin stepped onto some of the thickest carpet pile she'd ever felt. The apartment was lit with a warm, soft light. All the furnishings were obviously tremendously expensive, but arranged with care and good taste. She wondered what Luke would think of it all.

Her host was tall and thin, with a long, hooked nose and a full head of gray hair combed straight back. She pegged his age at about sixty. His posture was straight, no hint of a slouch. His eyes were dark and thoughtful. Overall, he was a little too serious to be good-looking. He reminded her of a retired college professor from some fancy ivy-league school. He wore a gray coat, waistcoat, and slacks, a white button-down shirt that looked like silk, and a maroon bow tie.

"Good evening... Miss O'Reilly?" He actually bowed to her and offered his hand.

"Officer Erin O'Reilly, sir," she said, shaking hands.

"I am delighted. If you would follow me?"

He ushered her into his living room. Erin sat carefully on the edge of a couch that probably cost more than her annual salary. She was starting to think it might have been a mistake to bring Rolf, but the Shepherd was well-behaved as always. He sat next to the couch and waited for instructions.

"What a remarkable animal," Clemenceau said. "May I presume he is employed by your department in an official capacity?"

"He's my partner," Erin said.

"Excellent," he said. "Would you care for a glass of wine? I have a very acceptable '64 Bersano."

She had no idea what that was, but it didn't matter. "I'm not allowed to drink on duty."

"Oh, of course," he said. "My apologies. Perhaps a cup of coffee, or tea?"

"Coffee would be fine."

"I fear it is not decaffeinated."

"That's fine," she said. "I'm not going to sleep for a while yet."

"The repose of sleep refreshes only the body," Clemenceau recited. "It rarely sets the soul at rest. The repose of the night does not belong to us. It is not the possession of our being. Sleep opens within us an inn for phantoms. In the morning we must sweep out the shadows."

"I'm sorry, what?"

"It has a more melodious sound in the original French," he said. "But I believe what Gaston Bachelard is saying is that when the mind is wakeful, sleep serves little purpose."

"Right," she said.

"Excuse me for one moment," he said, disappearing into the kitchen. While he put the coffee on, Erin looked around at what she could see from the couch. Clemenceau definitely had a fine collection of artwork, from about the same time period as the Madonna, and she was willing to bet they were originals.

The smell of fresh-roasted coffee wafted into the room, perking up her sleepy wits. A few minutes later, Clemenceau came back with a tray holding two cups, saucers, a sugar bowl, and a small pitcher of cream, all very carefully arranged. Erin reached for the cup, but he insisted on serving her.

"Cream, no sugar," she said. He poured and handed her a cup and saucer. She took a sip. It was easily the best coffee she'd had in months, maybe ever. She took another.

"Now, madam, what is the nature of your inquiry?" he asked, taking a sip of his own coffee.

"You know about the Madonna of the Water?" she asked.

"Indeed," he said. "Believed to be a Raphael. Quite lovely, by all accounts."

"Have you seen the painting?"

"Alas, no," he said. "As I am sure you are already aware, I attended the gala at the Queens Museum, but I foolishly believed there was no need for haste. I paid too much head to Jean Bruyère. He said, 'There is no road too long to the man who advances deliberately and without undue haste; there are no honors too distant to the man who prepares himself for them with patience.'"

"I don't think the thieves have read Jean What's-his-name," Erin said. "You know anything about the theft?"

"I?" Clemenceau raised his eyebrows. "I am shocked you would think such a thing of me, even on such short acquaintance. What have I ever done that would instill such suspicion?"

Luke had armed Erin for this moment. "The Titian that was stolen from Milan three years ago?" she suggested. "That ended up in your possession?"

For the first time in their conversation, Clemenceau looked a little uncomfortable. "A regrettable misunderstanding," he said. "I confess, in my eagerness to possess such a marvelous work, I neglected my research into the provenance of the item. I was insufficiently diligent. Since then, I have been more patient and circumspect."

"Right," Erin said, cutting through the bullshit. "You're saying you didn't know the painting was hot when you bought it. That's what you told Interpol when they called you. But you don't strike me as a guy who doesn't do his homework. You do everything neat and careful, even the little stuff. You expect me to believe you didn't ask any questions?"

He smiled thinly and stroked his chin. "The looks may belie the man, or the woman, for that matter. You have a keener eye than I had thought. But truly, I asked neither deep nor probing questions of the merchants of the painting to which you refer."

"Because you already knew the answers," she said. "Do you traffic in stolen paintings as a matter of habit?"

Clemenceau was still smiling, taking no offense. "Indeed not. I exert all legal means at my disposal to acquire that which I desire."

"And did you desire the Raphael?"

"Passionately."

"How passionately?"

"I anticipated with adolescent longing the titillation of the auction house," he said.

Erin couldn't believe this shit. Either he was trying to rattle her, or he really did talk this way. She decided to keep coming at him head-on. "Has Jake Gallagher offered you the painting?"

"I am sorry, madam, I have not the pleasure of that man's acquaintance."

"The painting thief. Did he offer to sell it to you?"

Clemenceau shook his head. "I fear not," he said sadly. "I fear, also, that these rough men may have damaged her with their mishandling. This whole affair is a terrible tragedy from beginning to end, made all the more poignant by the sacrifice of that noble policeman who fell attempting to thwart their evil designs."

"Yeah," Erin said, not knowing what else to say.

"In token of goodwill," he said, "and of the esteem in which I hold this fair city, I wish it known that, upon recovery of the Madonna in good condition, I shall make a small donation toward the upkeep and maintenance of the New York Police Department. Shall we say, one hundred?"

"A hundred bucks would be nice," she said.

"One hundred thousand dollars, Officer," he said gently.

"Oh."

"Now, have you any further questions on this or any other matter?"

Erin thought it over. This was getting her nowhere. "No," she said. She finished her coffee and stood up. He rose and walked her to the door. She gave him a card on her way out. "If you think of anything, or if anyone does contact you," she said.

"You shall be foremost in my thoughts," he said. Then, to her complete confusion, he bent over her hand and kissed the back of it. "I bid you good night, fair lady."

*   *   *

"Fair lady?" Erin repeated to Rolf as they drove south on 278. "*Fair lady?*"

Rolf didn't have anything to say on the subject.

"He's not the guy," she said to him, bouncing her thoughts off her partner. "He's crooked, sure. He'll buy stolen goods. But the way he talks about it... he needs to tell himself a story so he can sleep at night. And the story he tells is that he doesn't know for sure if a painting was illegally obtained. That way he can make believe his hands are clean. And that means he wouldn't hire guys to steal for him. Shit. I miss dealing with average street assholes. At least when they talk, I can understand them."

But she had two more art dealers to take care of. There was still a little evening left, and she intended to make use of it.

Chapter 17

Erin didn't have the room numbers at the Hilton, but the night clerk was very helpful when she flashed her shield. She tried Roy Atkins first, mainly because he was on the ninth floor and Dominique de Vere was up on Twelve. She took a deep breath and knocked.

"Mr. Atkins? NYPD. Please open up."

She waited. No answer.

After a few moments, she tried again. Still nothing. She leaned against the door, thinking maybe he had the TV or the shower on, but couldn't hear anything.

Either he was out, or he wasn't opening the door. In either case, there wasn't a thing she could do without a warrant, so she and Rolf moved on upstairs.

She knocked on de Vere's door. This time she didn't announce herself. It was only a legal requirement if she was serving a warrant, and she thought maybe there was a better chance of the door opening if they didn't know an officer was outside.

The door opened. Erin and the other person were both surprised. She was looking at a man of about forty. His hair was wet, like he'd just taken a shower, and he appeared to be wearing only a bathrobe. For his part, he'd clearly been expecting somebody else. They stared at one another for an awkward couple of seconds. He broke the silence first.

"You're not room service."

"You're not Ms. de Vere," she replied.

"Who is it, darling?" purred a female voice from inside.

"A woman... and a dog," he said over his shoulder.

"Sir," Erin said, "I'd like to talk to Dominique de Vere, please. My name is Officer O'Reilly. I'm with the NYPD."

He looked her over and liked what he saw. "You sure are," he said with a smile.

"Let her in," the woman said. "She sounds positively delightful."

The man stood to one side. As Erin walked in, Rolf beside her, she could feel the guy's eyes all over her. He closed the door behind her, and she was sure he was checking out her ass.

The room was part of a suite, one of the nicest in the hotel. The lights were turned down low. A woman was lounging on the couch. Her whole manner reminded Erin of a black cat relaxing. She was wearing a silky black nightdress. Her hair was black and lay loose around her shoulders. She was a little older than Erin and strikingly beautiful, with a model's high cheekbones and full, red lips. Erin distrusted her on sight.

"Ms. de Vere?" Erin asked.

The woman slowly, languidly straightened up. She adjusted her nightdress. It had ridden pretty far up her thighs. "I am. And you, my dear, are far too pretty to be a police officer."

"And your name, sir?" she asked the man, ignoring de Vere's last statement.

"I'm Roy Atkins," he said, extending his hand and smiling broadly. His teeth were very white and straight. "Please, call me Roy. You have a first name, O'Reilly?"

"Yeah, I do," she said.

He waited a second. She didn't tell him.

His grin didn't falter. "Okay, strictly business. I can respect that. I like a girl who knows what she wants. What're you drinking?" He moved toward the minibar.

"Mr. Atkins," she said. "I've been looking for you, too."

"Really?" He sounded pleased. "Hey, that's great, kid. Tell you what. Let's have a drink together, and we'll see if we can't all come out of this evening winners."

"Roy, darling," de Vere said. "Do you really think I want to share?"

"Hey, there's plenty to go round, babe," he said.

Erin was tired and didn't have time for this. "Ms. de Vere, Mr. Atkins," she began.

"Hey, babe, I told you, it's Roy," he said.

She didn't bother to answer that. "Both of you were at the Orphans of Europe gala at the Queens Museum," she said. "I'm interviewing people connected to the incident."

"Geez, kid, that's a big job," Atkins said. "There had to be a couple hundred people there. You getting to all of them in person? You've got to be exhausted. Have a seat, get comfortable. You sure you don't want that drink?"

He dropped to the couch and patted the cushion on one side of him. De Vere was on the other.

"No thanks," she said. She very deliberately sat in a chair to the side. Rolf gave Atkins a cool look and took up his usual place beside Erin.

"I'm coming to you because I hoped you could help with something," she said.

"Do go on," de Vere said. She slipped a hand inside Atkins's bathrobe and caressed his chest.

Erin felt a flush of embarrassment and irritation creeping onto her face. She was pretty sure de Vere was trying to make her uncomfortable on purpose, so she tried not to show any reaction. "We've caught almost all the thieves already," she said. "But the painting's still missing. We're going to get the last one. It's only a matter of time. But there's a concern that the painting may be damaged when we take him down."

She was bullshitting them, of course. While it was true that the NYPD would try not to damage the work of art, their main concern was neutralizing a cop-killer. All other concerns were a very distant second place.

"I'm glad to know your department is taking thought for such matters," de Vere said. "But I really don't see what we can do to help."

"There may be a possibility of negotiating the safe return of the painting," Erin said, improvising. "You have contacts in the New York art world. Would you be willing to help mediate a trade?"

"I think that's a great idea," Atkins said. "We don't want to risk more damage to such a unique work of art. Anything I can do to help, you've just got to ask. And let me say, I think the NYPD does a fantastic job. I mean that. You are the thin blue line, you know? On the one side we've got order, on the other is anarchy, and you're in between. I really respect that."

"Thanks," she said dryly. "Do either of you know where a thief would go to shift a stolen painting in New York?"

"Well, I really couldn't say," de Vere said. She leaned in close to Atkins and nuzzled his ear. "Unless, maybe..."

"You thinking the sheikh?" Atkins said. He seemed a little distracted by her attentions.

"Mmm," she murmured, doing something else with her hand inside his robe.

"The sheikh?" Erin asked.

Atkins didn't seem to be able to form a coherent response, but de Vere smiled at Erin.

"Omar Haddad," de Vere said. "The man has no principles."

"Yeah, I know about him," Erin said. She suddenly realized that she was done. A real detective would've kept at these two, pried some information loose from them. But she didn't wear a gold shield. She was just a patrol officer, tired, angry, and sick to death of these rich bastards. All she wanted to do was to climb in a shower and wash off the whole stinking mess, then sleep for two days straight.

She stood up abruptly. "Thanks for your time," she said. "I'll let you get back to your... evening. If you hear anything about the painting, will you let me know?" She laid a card on the end table.

"Of course," de Vere said.

Erin went to the door, opened it partway, and paused. "Oh, there's one more thing," she said, turning to face them. "How can I get in touch with Jake Gallagher?"

"Who?" Atkins said blankly. De Vere just raised her eyebrows.

"Okay, never mind," she said and got out of there. Her bed was waiting back at her apartment, and she didn't think she'd ever been so glad to know it was there.

Chapter 18

Erin was a morning person. No matter how tired she'd been the night before, she could never sleep in when something was on her mind. She slept soundly enough, but woke up just before seven with thoughts of the case running through her brain. There were leads she could still follow, but she had to be careful. Homicide was all over this case, and Lyons and Spinelli would be looking for an excuse to kick her to the curb again.

She wanted to hit the ground running, but breakfast was essential. Her dad had taught her never to start a long day on an empty stomach. She started the coffee pot and dropped two slices of bread into the toaster. While she waited, she fetched in the paper. The Internet might be the news source for the twenty-first century, but her memories of mornings with her dad and the New York Times were something she treasured. Sitting down at her dining table, she glanced at the headlines.

The newspaper fell from her fingers. "What the hell?" she murmured in disbelief. Her mouth hung open at the sight of the front page headline.

ALLEGED COP-KILLER SLAIN IN SHOOTOUT

Last night, just after midnight, the Queens ESU Tactical Unit stormed an apartment after receiving an anonymous tip that a suspected armed robber and slayer of an NYPD officer was present. A massive manhunt has been underway for Jacob Gallagher, 24, suspected in the daring heist of a Renaissance painting from the Queens Art Museum. Officer John Brunanski, 46, was mortally wounded when he attempted to thwart the robbers' escape. Mr. Gallagher is alleged to have worked with several accomplices, all of whom are now in police custody, according to a source in the department.

The same source states that the Tactical Unit acted on a so-called "no-knock warrant," meaning they broke forcefully into the apartment without warning. The details of the incident are still undergoing departmental review, but the source states that Mr. Gallagher brandished a pistol. The Tactical Unit officers fired rather than risk further police casualties.

Mr. Gallagher was taken to Queens Hospital, where he was pronounced dead on arrival from multiple gunshot wounds.

The NYPD is expected to release a press statement this morning. At the moment, the location of the stolen painting remains unknown, as does the identity of the officer or officers who fired the fatal shots. Per standard police procedure, those officers involved have been placed on administrative leave pending internal review of the shooting.

"A source in the department," Erin muttered. "I'll bet I know who. Detective goddamn Spinelli." She banged a fist on the table. The toaster ejected two pieces of crispy toast as if in answer. She knew how this was going to go. Her dad always said the right way to fight a war was to declare victory and go home. From Homicide's perspective, the case was now closed. Four men had participated in the shooting. Three had been arrested, one was dead. Simple enough.

But it wasn't that simple. The painting theft would be kicked over to Central Robbery Division, but they had a huge backlog of cases. It wouldn't be their chief priority. And where was the Madonna? Who had set up the heist in the first place? Erin ate quickly, dressed, and took Rolf outside. While he sniffed at fire hydrants and signposts, she tried to think.

The thieves must have already made delivery of the painting. That meant two things: one, that the mastermind was going to be hard to catch, especially if Gallagher was the only one who'd dealt with him; and two, if the police did manage to find the boss, they'd have incontrovertible evidence in the form of the painting itself. But to find that, they'd need a name and a search warrant, and that'd be hard to come by, especially now that the urgent pressure to catch the cop-killer was off.

The only real hope was that one of the other thieves, those still breathing, knew something the DA would be willing to trade for a sentence reduction. Otherwise, it was a dead end, the threads of the investigation neatly snipped off.

Erin paused, pulling Rolf up short on his leash. The Shepherd looked quizzically at her. "What if..." she began, trailing off into silence. Her partner waited patiently.

"It's awfully convenient," she said at last, "that an anonymous caller happens to bring the cops down on the last fugitive. Our guys went in primed for action. It doesn't take much to get a cop-killer shot. A tip that he's armed and dangerous... it's practically a setup for murder-by-cop."

That didn't prove anything by itself. Lots of cases broke on the basis of anonymous tips. That was one reason it was so important for a police force to be on good terms with the community it was trying to police. But still, it bothered her. The whole thing was just a little too tidy.

"Okay, boy," she said to Rolf. "Time to go back to work." It was Sunday, and her shift didn't start until Monday morning, but she was going in to the office. She needed access to the precinct, and with the press conference about to happen, she knew Lyons and Spinelli would be otherwise occupied for a while.

She stepped back inside for a moment, strapping on her Glock just in case. Then she was moving.

* * *

Erin was right about the precinct. There were a lot of cops and reporters around, but they were all clustered in the press room. The watch sergeant nodded a greeting to her, but she didn't meet anyone else as she headed for the computers. She didn't rate her own desktop machine, but Patrol Division had a few communal computers. She slid into a chair and started typing.

She knew she was risking her job. She'd been explicitly ordered off the case by the ranking detectives. She was interfering with an ongoing investigation. But Erin didn't care. She needed to see this through.

"*Sitz*, Rolf," she said, signaling him to a spot behind her chair. They had the room to themselves for now. If someone else showed up, Rolf would give her at least a little warning.

Erin brought up the case file on the Brunanski killing. She didn't have full access, but she scanned the information she could see. It wasn't much. She swore softly. There was only one thing she was really looking for, and it was sealed off in files only the case officers could get at. If she wanted those files, she needed to get into the Detective Bureau and onto Spinelli's computer.

She couldn't break into the Bureau. That wouldn't just get her fired; it could get her jail time. There had to be another way.

She drummed her fingers on the base of the keyboard, willing herself to think, damn it. Her dad, as straightforward a cop as ever there was, had told her, "You don't want to bang your head against a wall if you don't have to, kiddo. Go around the problem. There's no point kicking down a door when there's an open window just around the corner."

What she needed was a phone number. She couldn't get it from the case file. But maybe she could get it from the other side. She punched up the log of Dispatch calls. She had to look for patterns, since she could only see the numbers themselves, not the names attached to them. She could ask Dispatch, but that would put her on the record.

Erin didn't know exactly when the anonymous call had come in, but she knew what to look for. The moment it happened, the phone net would have caught fire. Calls would have gone out to Tactical, Detective Bureau, Patrol Division, the Precinct Captain's office, everybody. So she just needed to find the call that had opened the floodgates.

Nothing was ever that easy. Though she could see a massive spike in internal call volume Saturday evening, the 911 line for a city as big as Queens was constantly in use. Restricting herself to calls which had come in less than ten minutes before the alert went out, she still had half a dozen possibilities. And that was actually fewer than she could've expected. Erin sighed and brought up her reverse directory and an online map of Queens.

Two calls were from private residences. She checked the addresses against her directory. They appeared to be from ordinary citizens in blue-collar neighborhoods. Three others were from cell phones. If any of them were prepaid burners, they might be what she was looking for. But the sixth call had come from a pay phone. That by itself was unusual, in this day of smartphones. Erin was always a little surprised that phone booths still existed. She checked the reverse directory to locate the booth.

"Huh," she muttered, sitting back in her chair. "How about that."

She'd been expecting the booth to be on the street, near the apartment where Jake Gallagher's life had ended. But it was a phone in the lobby of the Crowne Plaza Hotel, next to JFK Airport.

Erin did a quick cross-check and saw that no police had responded to the Crowne Plaza. Whatever had led someone to call 911 from the hotel, it hadn't resulted in any officers showing up there.

"That's gotta be it," she told Rolf, who looked suitably impressed with her police work. "So how does someone at the hotel know about an armed fugitive hiding out in an apartment halfway across town?"

The problem was, the call had come from a lobby phone. Anyone could have made the call, including a guest, or someone just passing through on their way...

"On their way to the airport," she whispered. "No. Dammit, no!"

Erin leaped out of the chair and ran from the room. Rolf scrambled to his feet and trotted after her. As she sprinted out of the station toward her car, she glanced at the clock above the front desk. It read 8:50.

"Where's the fire, O'Reilly?" the watch sergeant called after her. She didn't bother to answer. She might already be too late.

* * *

Erin took the Long Island Expressway to the Van Wyck Expressway. Thanking God for the light early-Sunday traffic, she flipped on her flashers and siren, pushing the Charger as hard as she dared. Other drivers made rude gestures at the police cruiser, in typical New York fashion, but they got out of her way. Rolf, in his quick-release box, was alert and attentive. They were chasing something, and he wanted a piece of the action.

She exited to Van Wyck Boulevard and throttled down to a speed that was only a little bit crazy. Her tires squealed as she hung a hard left onto 133rd Avenue and crossed the Expressway eastbound. She took another sharp turn, south on 140th Street, and hurtled down the residential street. She and Rolf both noticed a woman walking a German Shepherd who paused to stare at them. Then she was coming up on the turn to 135th Avenue and the hotel. She put on the brakes and turned off the lights and siren. It wouldn't do to scream into the hotel parking lot like a demon if her quarry was still inside.

She parked, released Rolf, and jogged across the lot to the hotel lobby. As she reached the doors, she remembered that she wasn't in uniform. She'd dressed in her usual off-duty clothes, slacks and a dark blue blouse. At least she had her shield and gun.

The clerk at the front desk looked fresh-faced, clean-scrubbed, and helpful. "Good morning, ma'am!" he said brightly. "How may I—"

She cut him off by holding up her wallet, flashing her shield. "NYPD, sir. I need to see your guest list right away."

His smile faltered. "Ma'am—officer—I really need to talk to my manager about this. If you could just hold on a moment, I can call him and—"

"We have reason to believe a dangerous fugitive is currently staying here," she interrupted. "I need to see the list *now*."

"I don't know," the clerk said, blinking rapidly. "I think I'm supposed to see a court order, or a warrant, or something."

Erin held her rising temper in check. "I just need to know if the guy's still here, or if he's checked out."

"Certainly, ma'am," he said, recovering a bit. "What's the name?"

Erin froze. She still didn't know who she was chasing. Thinking quickly, and running down her list of suspects, she said, "He could be using an alias. He could be under Adlai Martin, Roy Atkins, Phineas Van Ormond... or Schenk. Rudolf Schenk."

"Just a second," the clerk said. He was much happier to look for specific names than to give unfettered computer access to a cop without official paperwork. His fingers clicked rapidly on the keyboard, but to Erin the time dragged agonizingly.

"I don't see..." he said. Erin closed her eyes and lowered her head. "Wait!"

Erin's heart skipped a beat.

"Got it!" he said triumphantly. He pivoted the monitor and showed it to her. There was a familiar name.

"Yes, good, great," Erin said. "Has he checked out yet?"

"No. He's still there. Looks like he called up room service just a few minutes ago. I guess he's having breakfast in his room."

"What's the room number?" Erin demanded.

"He's in one of the Executive Suites," the clerk said. "On the tenth floor, Room Ten-oh-Five. Ma'am, please don't cause any trouble here. We need to preserve our reputation and—"

Erin was already halfway to the elevator, Rolf right beside her.

Chapter 19

Erin spent the elevator ride thinking about her next move. The main question was, should she call for backup? On the one hand, this could be the most important bust of her career. If something happened to her, the mastermind would get away. At the moment, she was the only cop who had any idea what was going on. But what was going to happen? She was on her way to confront an art collector, not a desperado. And she had her partner with her. She looked fondly down at Rolf, wondering whether any human partner would have followed her into this mess as willingly. And she was supposed to be off the case. If she called backup, there'd be a lot of explaining to do. Besides, what if she was wrong? What if she called in the cavalry for nothing?

The elevator bell chimed as the car came to a smooth stop. She unconsciously put her hand on the butt of her Glock. But this was a highly-rated New York hotel, not a gang's headquarters. There were no thugs standing guard in the hallway. In fact, it was totally empty. The style of décor was modern and off-putting to her working-class sensibilities, all cold grays and whites with the occasional splash of brilliant crimson. The carpets had an odd design of black lines on gray, forming geometric patterns that reminded her of spider webs.

She moved down the hall, checking room numbers until she came to 1005. The door was closed, of course, and she couldn't help but smile at the little white "Do Not Disturb" sign in the keycard slot.

Erin raised her hand to knock, and then hesitated. What was the best way to do this? Play it cool, pretend not to know what was going on, get invited in? What reason could she give for being there? No, he'd remember she was a cop. And without a warrant, she couldn't legally enter the room without permission. She needed probable cause, and at the moment, she didn't have it.

She could just kick the door in and storm the suite. That was if she wanted to end the day without her shield, her gun, or her future, having traded them all in for a couple of lawsuits the perp and the Crowne Plaza would have filed against the New York Police Department. The case would be thrown out before she could see straight.

She looked down at Rolf again and had to laugh at herself. She was a K-9 officer, all right. She'd come up against that most insurmountable of obstacles to even the best-trained dog—a closed door.

Her best bet was probably to find a place where she could watch the door and just wait. He couldn't stay in there forever, and she had nowhere else to be. Follow him downstairs, or better yet, get in the elevator and take him quietly into custody. After all the rush and hurry to get to the hotel, it went against everything in her gut, but maybe patience was what was called for.

Erin turned to retreat, and then paused. The inquisitive little girl in her made her lean carefully against the door, pressing her ear to the wood. She didn't expect anything, maybe the sound of the TV, but she was hoping to hear something that would convince her the suspect was still inside.

She heard a voice. It was guttural, harsher, and definitely angry. And it belonged to Rudolf Schenk.

"—sort of man do you think me? You think this is about the money? It was never about the money!"

Another voice answered, much more quietly. She couldn't make it out, but thought it had an English accent. In any case, Schenk didn't let the other finish.

"Yes, I know you will run now. But I was right about you, *Herr Doktor*. I told the police *Fräulein* of my suspicions."

"You did *what*?"

Those words were loud enough for Erin to recognize the other speaker. It was Phineas Van Ormond, and his voice had lost its cool.

"*Ja*, I spoke with her yesterday. She is more clever than I thought, and more clever than you, I think. She will find you out, and—"

Apparently Van Ormond had heard enough, because the next sound Erin heard, even muffled by the door, was unmistakable. It was the crack of a pistol shot. Schenk's voice cut off into a grunt.

Erin jumped back from the door, one hand instinctively reaching for a police radio that wasn't there, the other unsnapping the safety strap on her Glock. She drew the gun, chambered a round, and held it pointed at the door while she backed away and fumbled out her phone with her left hand. She keyed Dispatch on speed-dial without a moment of hesitation. The equation had just changed. She now had probable cause, an armed felon, and a man who was either dead or wounded on the other side of the door. The cavalry couldn't get there fast enough for her.

"Dispatch."

"Officer O'Reilly, shield four-six-four-oh," she said, speaking quickly and quietly. She took a breath and ran through the list of signal codes. "I've got a 10-34S at the Crowne Plaza, Room ten-oh-five. This is a 10-13Z. Suspect is Van Ormond, Phineas." The codes indicated a violent assault in progress, with shots fired, and an officer in civilian clothes requesting assistance.

"Ten-four, O'Reilly," came Dispatch's unflappable answer. "Units inbound, ETA five to ten."

"I also need a 10-54S forthwith," Erin added, indicating a serious ambulance case. "Am entering to render assistance."

"Ten-four, O'Reilly," Dispatch said again. "Exercise caution."

Erin wasn't about to exercise anything but her leg. She gauged the distance to the door, cocked her foot, and kicked the door right next to the knob. She'd been hoping for cheap veneer over hollow core, but this door was exactly the hardwood it appeared to be. She could no more kick it to pieces than she could punch through a brick wall. Fortunately, the doorframe was another story. Erin was glad she wasn't bursting into a drug den. Those guys knew how to reinforce a door. This hotel was built for show, so the guests could feel the reassuring solidity of the door as they closed it for the night. The receiving slot for the latch and lock was held in place by a thin strip of wood that gave way at once, tearing completely free of the wall and flying into the room in a shower of splinters. The door swung open so hard it hit the wall and began to bounce back again.

"Police! Hands in the air!" she ordered, charging into the room, tracking for a target with her eyes and Glock. "Rolf, *geh rein! Fass!*"

Rolf leapt past her with a snarl, his training homing in on the command to charge and bite. Erin realized she'd made a procedural mistake. When in doubt, her instructors always told her, send the dog in first. Your life is more important than his. But when Rolf was on duty, he had his vest. Now he didn't. So she'd gone first.

Heart pounding, Erin took in the room in a series of fractured images. The executive suite had a living-room area, with a desk at one end and a two-seat leather couch at the other. On the couch, slumped as though sleeping, was Schenk. His suit coat was open and the white of his shirtfront was turning red just below the sternum. Erin couldn't tell whether he was alive or dead.

To one side was a bathroom and a kitchenette, to the other the bedroom. Rolf was making for the bedroom, but even as he rushed the doorway and Erin pivoted to cover him, the door slammed shut. Rolf sprang at it, scrabbling with his paws at the doorknob, barking and growling in frustration.

"I know you're in there, Van Ormond!" Erin shouted. "This is the police! Open the door and throw the gun out, then come out with your hands in the air!"

There was a brief pause. "No, dear girl, I don't think I shall," came Van Ormond's answer. He'd recovered his polish. The man sounded like he was talking over tea in an English country house, rather than barricaded in a hotel room with a cop outside and a man he'd just shot on the couch.

"There's nowhere to run, Professor," she said. "We're on the tenth floor, and this is the only door. Either you come out, or we come in and get you."

"I shall be coming out," Van Ormond said. "But in my own time and in my own manner, thank you."

"There's only two ways this ends," she said, gritting her teeth. "Either you leave this building in handcuffs, or you leave in a body bag. Your choice."

"Call off your dog, and I shall emerge," he promised. "*Fräulein.*"

Erin started. Schenk was struggling to sit upright. His complexion, never healthy, was ghastly white.

"Stay still, Doctor," she said. "An ambulance is coming."

"*Fräulein*, take care," Schenk whispered. "He is... very dangerous."

"No shit," she muttered. Rolf was still leaping at the door, growling ferociously. "Okay, Van Ormond, here's my offer," she said more loudly. "I get my dog to stand back. Then you come out slowly. If you have a gun in your hand, if you try anything at all, Rolf tears your balls off and I shoot you right in the face. Deal?"

"My dear girl, this is hardly the tone in which to conduct a delicate negotiation," the professor said. "Very well, Miss O'Reilly. I shall do as you ask."

"I'm not your dear fucking girl," she snapped. Erin didn't trust him, but she couldn't render first aid to Schenk with an armed man in the next room, and the wounded man was obviously fading. Where was the damn backup? Still eight minutes out, probably. That was eight minutes Schenk didn't have.

"Rolf. *Hier!*" she ordered.

The Shepherd heeded the command, coming back to her side.

"*Bleib!*" she ordered, the German for "stay." Her partner obediently stood fast, but his hackles were raised and a low growl rumbled in his chest. "Okay, Van Ormond, come on out. Slow and careful, or I'll shoot."

The doorknob turned and the door gradually opened. Erin held her pistol in both hands, sighting along the barrel, and remembered her instructors' advice. When in doubt, put two in the chest and one in the head. If the target didn't go down, keep shooting until he did. Don't take chances. She tried to breathe slowly and deeply, wondering if she could do it. She'd never fired at a living person.

A face came into view. But it wasn't Van Ormond's. It was an unnaturally peaceful woman, smiling with the benign good faith of a saint. Erin was staring at the Madonna of the Water. Van Ormond was holding the painting in front of himself as a shield.

The little cabinet painting was much too small to cover the portly professor's bulky body, but it did exactly what Van Ormond had intended. Erin hesitated, shifting aim. In that moment, the Englishman's other hand came out from behind the painting. He was holding a little pistol, a Walther PPK automatic. Some disconnected part of Erin's mind recognized it as the gun James Bond used. *How cliché*, she thought. It was pointed directly at her.

"Rolf, *fass!*"

Erin hadn't gotten the words out. They'd come from the wounded man on the couch. Schenk, the German, had managed to force a commanding tone from his punctured body as he called to the dog in his native language.

Rolf was a police dog, trained to respond to his partner's commands, not those of a random bystander. But in this case, the man was telling him to do something Erin had told him to do just a few moments before, and it was something he wanted to do very badly. The German Shepherd's powerful legs coiled into a spring, carrying him across the open space of the living room in less than a second. Van Ormond's finger reflexively tightened on the Walther's trigger, but the gun wavered halfway between Erin and her dog and the bullet whistled past her to bury itself in the wall. The professor had no time for a second shot. Rolf went for the weapon arm, exactly as he'd been trained, and bit. His powerful jaws clamped down on muscle and bone, even as the impact of his charging body forced the arm out and to the side. The professor sat down heavily, dropping the painting. He held onto the pistol a moment longer, muscles contracting involuntarily as Rolf's teeth sank deeper, and another harmless shot skimmed the carpet into the baseboard. Then the Walther dropped from his hand.

Erin took two steps forward, clearing her line of fire to aim over her dog at Van Ormond's pudgy, sweating face. She kicked the fallen handgun away even as she heard the first sirens, distant but closing fast.

"Phineas Van Ormond," she said, "You're under arrest for attempted murder, assaulting a police officer, armed robbery, receiving stolen goods... oh, Christ, I don't know. A whole lot of other shit, too. I'll read you your rights in a second. Right now, you have the right to stay the hell where you are. If you move, I really will have Rolf tear off your balls."

The art collector's shoulders slumped in defeat. Rolf, still growling, kept his grip on the man's arm but didn't inflict any further damage. Erin scooped up the Walther and did a quick check on Van Ormond to ensure he didn't have any other weapons. Then she hurried to Schenk's side. The German's breathing was labored and faint. Erin probed his injury. The bullet had missed his heart, but she guessed he had a pneumothorax injury—an air bubble in his chest that had partially collapsed one of his lungs. He was bleeding heavily and only semiconscious.

"It's okay, Doctor," she said. "I'll take care of you." But there wasn't much she could do without a chest tube. Where the hell were the EMTs? "The ambulance will be here any minute. Just hang on."

Schenk smiled faintly. "I told you... that you would not rest... until you found... your man," he whispered. "Let me... see... her."

For a moment Erin couldn't think what he meant. Then she scrambled across the room and snatched up the fallen painting.

"See, Dr. Schenk, here's the Madonna. She's fine. We've saved her." As she held up the ancient canvas, Erin saw to her dismay that she'd left bloody fingerprints on the upper portion of the painting. "Oh shit, I'm sorry."

"Do not worry, *Fräulein*," he replied. "Blood can be... cleaned away." His eyes were only half-open, but he stared at his family's lost heirloom with undiminished love. "She... is... so beautiful." His eyes closed and his head fell away to the side, that faint smile still tracing his lips.

"No, damn it!" Erin shouted, grabbing his shoulder as if she could shake more life into him. "Not again! You don't get to die on me, Schenk, you sour son of a bitch! You're stronger than this! You're too goddamn grumpy to die! You hear me?"

She was still talking, almost babbling, when the backup arrived. Two uniformed officers entered with guns drawn. The ambulance crew was close behind them. One of the officers drew Erin away from the wounded man while the other took Van Ormond into custody and the EMTs went to work. Erin stood back, staring numbly down at the priceless painting in her hands, her fingerprints etched in blood on the canvas. The Madonna smiled placidly, her expression as calm and forgiving as it had been when the Renaissance master had first painted it. Erin kept staring at it as she backed up to the wall and slid down to the floor.

Chapter 20

The press conference was long over by the time Erin got Van Ormond back to the precinct. She was booking him when Lyons and Spinelli came looking for her. Her call for backup had identified her, she was off-duty and somewhere she had no business being, and the detectives, for all their faults, weren't total morons.

"What the hell were you doing, O'Reilly?" Spinelli snapped.

Erin was too tired to even try to play games with these two. "I was doing my job," she shot back. "No, wait. That's not right. I was doing *your* job."

Spinelli was so angry he just spluttered, his mouth opening and closing. Lyons stepped toward her threateningly. "You stupid bitch," he growled. "You'll lose your shield for this."

"For what?" Erin exploded. "For stopping a murder? For recovering stolen property? I was being a cop, for God's sake!"

"You should have told us what you knew," Spinelli said, recovering a little.

"You didn't want my help!" Erin retorted. "You made that plenty clear. By the time you finished showing off for the reporters, it wouldn't have mattered anyway. Schenk would've been dead and this guy," she prodded a dejected and bloodstained Van Ormond, "would've been on a plane back to England. He had the boarding pass in his pocket."

"There's a chain of command, Officer," Spinelli said coldly. "And you went around it. You interfered with a major investigation. You've been insubordinate, unruly, and reckless. You put yourself and others in danger. And you're going to regret it." He turned and stalked off. Lyons, with a final glare, followed.

"Hey, guys," Erin called after them. "I got the painting back. Just thought you might like to know, so you can announce it to the press."

Spinelli's shoulders twitched. He just kept walking.

"O'Reilly?"

Erin gritted her teeth and turned, ready for another fight. But it was just Porter, her fellow Patrol Officer. "What's up?" she asked.

"Murphy wants to see you, as soon as you're finished here," Porter said. She looked Van Ormond up and down. "That's him, huh?"

"Yeah," Erin said. "You done, Sarge?"

"Just about," the booking sergeant said. "You just need to sign."

Erin scribbled her name on the arrest report and took the long walk to her Lieutenant's office. She tried to think how it was going to go. Had she gotten him in trouble? Had she just flushed away her whole career?

Murphy was behind his desk, no trace of a smile on his usually-jovial face. "Come in, Officer," he said. "Close the door."

Heart pounding, Erin did as she was told. She came to attention in front of his desk and braced herself.

The Lieutenant sighed. "O'Reilly, you really stepped in it," he said. "Spinelli's filed an incident report over the shootout you and Paulson got in at that construction site. Now you go and grab a suspect, without a warrant, and he's a foreign national? This just got political, kiddo."

"I had PC," Erin protested. "I heard the gunshot and—"

Murphy held up his hand. "Okay, okay. Save it. I'm on your side, believe it or not. You did what you thought you had to, and I understand you got the painting back. I just called the hospital, and it sounds like Dr. Schenk's going to make it. So you saved his life. But this is going to a board of inquiry. I can't stop that." He sighed again. "I hate like hell to have to say this, O'Reilly. But pending the board's review, you're suspended from duty, with pay. I need your shield and gun."

Erin wanted to scream at him, to protest, but all her anger had drained out of her. This was it, end of career. Wordlessly, she unbuckled her Glock and slid it across the desk. She reached for her shield and laid it down beside the gun.

"Go home, O'Reilly," Murphy said. "You look like you could use a rest."

*   *   *

But Erin couldn't rest. She called Luke, as she'd promised. He met her outside her apartment. "Erin, what happened?" were his first words when he saw her face.

"Let me put Rolf up," she said. "Then I need a drink. I'm not saying another word until I've got a glass in my hand."

They went to the Priest. Luke got a beer, and Erin ordered a Black Velvet.

"So," he said when their drinks arrived, "what happened?"

"It was your guy, Luke," she said. "It was Van Ormond."

He blinked. "What do you mean?"

She took a deep breath. "We haven't done the interrogation yet, but here's what they're going to find. Van Ormond came over from England for the Madonna. He's an out-of-town guy without any underworld connections, so he hired some local boys for the heist. I'm guessing he only worked through Jake Gallagher, so the others wouldn't see his face or know his name. He gave them the job, and I'll give Gallagher credit, they did it like pros. They learned about the extra security for the gala and figured it was an opportunity. They found out what uniforms the guards at the museum would be wearing and stole four of them from a local store. That was their first mistake. They should've just bought or rented them. I nabbed Cal Huntington at the scene of the robbery and found out some rent-a-cop outfits were missing. Still, if I hadn't been at the gala, maybe no one would've put it together.

"Of course, if I hadn't made the crooks, Brunanski wouldn't have gotten shot," she added. She took a gulp of her drink, feeling the champagne burn in her throat, and went on.

"With one of the gang wounded, and a cop dead, they went into panic mode and scattered. I'll bet Gallagher sold them some BS about how he'd pay them off once the heat died down. Maybe it wasn't even bullshit and he really did mean to look after his guys. We'll never know. We started scooping them up one by one. Huntington gave up the other gang members, and pretty soon we had everyone but Gallagher.

"He was the brains of the gang, though, and he'd gone to ground away from his usual stomping grounds. I think we'd have gotten him anyway, in just a couple of days, and Van Ormond thought so, too. They got in touch to finish the deal. Van Ormond got the painting, Gallagher got his payoff. Then Van Ormond tipped off the cops and we killed Gallagher."

"Wait a minute," Luke said. "If Van wanted Gallagher dead, why pay him? Why not just shoot him?"

"At that point, Van Ormond still hadn't shot anyone," Erin said. "He may have preferred to keep his hands as clean as possible. He probably wishes he'd just gunned Gallagher down.

But killing someone is a big deal, and even bad guys usually try to avoid it. I think he had second thoughts, but by then it was too late. So he gambled and called the police, told them Gallagher was armed and dangerous, and basically used the NYPD as his personal hit squad. If ESU had been a little less trigger-happy, he might've been in trouble, but his plane was about to leave. At that point, it was either roll the dice or spend the rest of his life looking over his shoulder.

"It was a big risk, but it paid off. Now Van Ormond had the painting, no one could ID him, and he had a ticket out of New York. All he had to do was sit tight for a few hours, and he'd be home free. But he didn't reckon on Schenk. I still don't know how Schenk made him. I'll have to talk to him. If I'd believed him at first, I could've stopped him from getting shot. That's on me, too."

"And me," Luke said ruefully. "I'm the one who told you it couldn't be Van. I'm still having trouble believing it."

"Schenk showed up at Van Ormond's hotel room, right as he was getting ready to leave," she continued. "That must've been awkward. But nothing Van Ormond couldn't handle. Schenk's no good at diplomacy. He said something stupid and confrontational. Van Ormond had a gun, just in case, and blam, problem solved. Except that he'd made one last mistake. He'd gotten a little careless and called in the tip about Gallagher from his own hotel lobby. If he'd used a phone somewhere closer to the hideout, I think he'd have gotten away with it. It's the little things that catch big-time crooks, that's what my dad says.

"I got there just in time, heard the shot, busted in, and almost got myself killed," she finished. "I wasn't expecting him to use the Madonna as a human shield. Not a human shield, exactly, but you know what I mean."

"He hid behind the painting?" Luke said, eyes wide.

"Yeah," she said. "He figured I wouldn't shoot up a priceless work of art just to take down a bad guy."

"Was he right?"

Erin stared at her half-empty glass and thought about her answer. "No," she said at last. "No, I would've put him down. If I hadn't, Schenk and I both would've died, and maybe Rolf too. Schenk might've been willing to die for the Madonna, but I wasn't about to let him. But I did hesitate. Just for a second, and it damn near killed me."

"So Van shot at you?"

"He missed, and Rolf took him down," she said. "Schenk knew Rolf was a German-trained dog, who knew German commands, and he told him to attack. It's a good thing my partner didn't freeze like I did. Rolf broke Van Ormond's gun arm. That dog's got a bite like you wouldn't believe."

"Wow," Luke said.

"Here's the thing, Luke," she went on. "You talk about how much respect Van Ormond has for art. If that'd been true, he wouldn't have put the Madonna in danger like that. Not even to save his own skin. I don't think he ever intended to keep her."

"What did he want, then?" Luke asked.

"The money," she said. "At the gala, I saw his suit was looking a little frayed around the edges. The more a guy talks about how money doesn't matter to him, the more you can bet it's what he really cares about. When we run his financials, I'm betting we find some hefty debts."

"Who would have been his buyer?"

She shrugged. "Take your pick. Any one of these sleazebags would've jumped at the chance to make a private sale instead of taking their chances at auction. They'd be guaranteed to end up with her, and they'd pay less. Luke, I don't know how you live in that world."

"This from the woman who chases criminals 24/7," Luke said. He took a long pull at his beer and grimaced, clearly wishing for something stronger. "At least the art dealers don't shoot each other. Usually. So what happens now?"

"Now?" Erin laughed bitterly. "Now I go before the Board and they decide whether or not to fire me. Then, if I've still got a job, I work Patrol until I retire, because as long as Spinelli's in the Bureau I'm sure as hell never making Detective. He'll hate me for going behind his back on this and spoiling the biggest case of his career."

"I guess you won, though," Luke said. "Good work, Erin. And thanks for sharing the drink." He stood up from the bar.

"Where are you going?" she asked, confused.

"There's some stuff I need to take care of, job-related," he said. "And I need to think this over. I'll call you. Thanks again." But he didn't meet her eyes.

Erin sat alone at the bar, finishing her Velvet. When it was done, she ordered another.

* * *

Erin didn't know what to do with herself. She worked with Rolf a lot, honing his training and trying not to think about the fact that if she lost her job, she'd lose him too. She cleaned her apartment, watched movies, read the papers. That was probably a mistake, since they were filled with nonsense about the case—*her* case. Her name wasn't even mentioned. Someone at the precinct, Spinelli probably, had managed the news output so the cop who'd arrested Van Ormond was described as "An off-duty New York Police Officer." They didn't even mention Rolf. It would all come out in the end, but by then her career would be in the toilet and the public would have moved on.

She felt completely alone. Luke didn't call, and she didn't dare contact him, remembering the troubled look in his eyes at their last meeting. She could have called on her family, but it would've gotten back to her dad, and that was one thing she couldn't face. He'd been a beat cop his whole career, had never made Detective, but he'd been good police, reliable, dependable. He'd sure as hell never gone before a Board of Inquiry. The thought of hearing the disappointment in his voice was too much for her.

If Erin wasn't a cop, she wasn't anything. It was the only thing she'd ever wanted to be. And if they took her shield, they'd take Rolf. They'd give him to another officer. That was the worst of it.

She was slipping into depression. The only good thing was that she knew it. She stayed off alcohol, for the most part, and her daily walks with Rolf got her out of the apartment and reminded her there was a world out there. But she needed a lifeline.

Finally, four days into her suspension, it hit her. There was someone she could see, someone who knew the truth. And he was someone she'd meant to visit anyway. She shook herself together, dressed with a little more care than she'd used the last few days, and headed to the hospital.

Chapter 21

Rudolf Schenk wasn't rich, but he was a foreign VIP and that made him important enough to rate a private room. Erin's first thought on entering was that it was awfully empty for the room of a man who'd very nearly been shot to death. There were no flowers, no get-well cards, and no other visitors. Schenk lay alone, his gaunt face even hollower than she remembered it, a blue pastel hospital gown hanging loosely on his bony frame. A medical machine stood beside the bed, covered with indicator lights, connected to the man by a clip on his fingertip. Every couple of seconds it gave an ambiguous beep.

Erin paused in the doorway, suddenly uncertain. She lifted a hand and tentatively tapped on the door.

"*Fräulein* O'Reilly," Schenk said, turning to her and smiling. It was a genuine smile, surprising in its warmth, and Erin felt a sudden rush of gratitude. She so desperately needed to see a friendly face that his gladness drew her like a magnet.

"How are you, Dr. Schenk?" she asked, stepping inside.

"I am well, thanks to you," he said. "The operation was successful. The surgeon removed the bullet from my chest, and he believes I will make a full recovery in time. You saved my life, *Fräulein*."

"We saved each other," she said, "and Rolf saved both of us."

"Yes, your excellent hound," Schenk said. "He is not with you, I see."

"It's a hospital," she said. "I didn't think the doctors would like it."

"Yes, you are correct," he said. "The doctors, nothing pleases them. All the same, I would like to see him again. I think I shall give him a token of gratitude. A fine steak, perhaps?"

Erin grinned. "If you do that, you'll have made a friend for life."

"And how goes it with you, *Fräulein*?"

"I'm okay," she said unconvincingly.

Schenk's gaze sharpened. "What has happened?" he asked, sitting up, then sagging back with a wince.

"Nothing," she said.

He waited, like a teacher who knows a student hasn't done her homework, saying nothing.

"It's just all going wrong," she burst out. "Everything. The painting got wrecked, you got shot, the detectives hate me, they've taken away my shield and... and they'll probably take my dog." To her horror, she realized she was in danger of breaking down in tears.

Schenk waited until she ran out of breath. If he had spoken kindly and softly, she would have lost it completely. Instead, he rubbed his chin and stared at her with cool, clinical eyes. "*Fräulein* O'Reilly," he said, "you are a good policewoman. You followed your clues and, even more, your instincts. You caught your thief and recovered his prize. You saved me from death. You did what none other in your police force could do. You did all this, and you ask for my pity? I refuse. What I give you is my respect."

Erin sank into the room's only chair. "I don't need your respect," she said.

"Of course you do," he retorted. "Everyone needs respect, from oneself. If you have your self-respect, you laugh at the others."

"Easy for you to say," she said. "Those others can throw me off the force."

Schenk shrugged, and then winced again. "But they cannot take away what you did. You avenged your fellow policeman. Did you not know when you set out the price you might pay?"

She sighed. "Yeah, I just thought I could get away without paying it."

He smiled again. "And you claim to believe in justice."

Erin had to laugh a little at the dark humor of that. "Everyone believes in justice—until it's our own ass on the line," she said.

Schenk joined in her laugh, though it clearly hurt him to do so. "Well said! So let there be no more self-pity. Let us think instead of what you have achieved. Do not worry about the blood on the painting, it is nothing. Fresh blood can be easily cleaned from paint. And the restorers of paintings, they have done more. I have learned they have cleaned the blood of my uncle from the Madonna as well, while they were about it. They have taken the blood away for testing, and she is cleansed from all stains. She will be placed again on exhibit, back at your museum, in three days' time."

"Yeah, I saw that in the paper," Erin said. "I'm glad I didn't ruin it—her, I mean. She's beautiful."

"Yes," Schenk said wistfully. "She is. I would like to see her again." He looked at her with a gleam almost of mischief in his eyes. "*Fräulein* O'Reilly, you are in trouble for breaking the rules, *ja*? Will you help me by breaking another?"

"What did you have in mind, Doctor?" she asked, though she already had an idea.

"An escape," he said. "I am to be kept prisoner here two to three weeks longer, so the surgeon says. But what does he know? I am old and tough. I will be able to go out for a short while, if I have a caretaker. And I must see the Madonna again. What say you?"

Erin held up a hand. "Dr. Schenk, I'm not going to break you out of the hospital. You're grouchy enough; you just might keel over and die on me. If you want out, I'll see what I can do, but we're bringing a nurse. That's not negotiable."

"As you wish, *Fräulein*," he said. "I leave it in your most capable hands."

"Dr. Schenk, I have a question," she said, changing the subject. "What were you doing at Van Ormond's apartment?"

It was Schenk's turn to sigh. "I was foolish," he said. "I lost patience with you and your department. I wished to confront him before he left for England. I told him I knew he had stolen the Madonna, and that I would be watching him for all time. I told him he would not have a moment's peace from me."

"That wasn't very smart," Erin agreed. "Didn't you realize how much danger you were putting yourself in?"

"I knew the man was capable of theft, but murder? I underestimated him. When he produced his pistol I recognized my error, but it was by then too late. I was too angry to stop, and I continued to promise revenge upon him. Then he shot me," he finished ruefully.

"Don't feel too bad about it," Erin said. "The most common last words a guy says when he's facing down a gunman are 'You don't have the guts!'"

Schenk nodded. "Our species rushes always toward self-destruction," he said. "As individuals, and also as a whole."

"On that note," she said, "I'd love to take you to see some art. After all, it's just a trip to the museum. What could possibly go wrong?"

"Please, *Fräulein*, have pity," he said. "It pains me to laugh."

*   *   *

As far as great escapes went, it wasn't going to make any headlines. Erin worked within the rules, despite what Schenk had said, and talked to his surgeon. She explained how important the painting was to the German, suggesting that it would help his recovery to see it. Finally, the doctor agreed to a short outing, but only in a wheelchair, with a trained nurse present at all times, and only for an hour.

With nothing better to do, bored and restless, Erin bought herself a new dress. This was an unusual thing for her, but she found herself in an unusual situation with a lot of spare time on her hands. Besides, her last formal dress had been ruined. The bloodstains would never come out, and the hem had gotten torn. Her new dress was black, as a kind of memorial for John Brunanski. All the same, this didn't really look like a mourning dress. Its velvet hugged her tightly, with lace panels on the sides, and showed off what she knew were her best assets, her arms and legs. It was high at the neck but left her shoulders bare, and the ankle-length skirt was slit high up her left thigh. She wore high-heeled ankle boots to finish off the ensemble.

She knew the dress was a success when she went to fetch Dr. Schenk. A male orderly, carrying a clipboard, walked straight into a support pillar when she passed him. Even Schenk, the dour professor, favored her with an appreciative look. His nurse had helped him dress in a dark, conservative suit, complete with a black bow tie. He was already in his wheelchair, waiting for her. *Good Lord*, Erin thought. *I look like his damn trophy wife!*

The nurse, a pleasant middle-aged Hispanic woman named Luisa, wheeled him down the hall, through the lobby, and out into the cool evening air. It was a little after nine, and the exhibition started at 9:30.

Chapter 22

Erin had a shiver of remembrance, almost a flashback, as they entered the museum. She instinctively glanced at the security personnel and was glad to see half a dozen NYPD uniforms along with the rent-a-cops. Clearly, no one was risking a repeat of the gala. The place was at least as crowded as it had been for the first opening, the ranks of art aficionados padded with a fair number of reporters. Luisa pushed Schenk's wheelchair around the edge of the atrium, keeping him out of the thickest part of the crowd.

Then Erin saw a particular shape among the guests, a very tall, grim, dark-skinned man, and beside him, sporting a pair of crutches, another familiar figure. And they were headed her direction. "Oh, come on," she said quietly.

Omar Haddad somehow managed to make his limping stride look graceful. He drew up in front of her, leaned on his left crutch, handed his right to Ibrahim, and extended his hand to her. In the absence of polite alternatives, she accepted it. He brought her hand smoothly up to his lips and brushed the back of it with a kiss.

"Good evening, Miss O'Reilly," he said softly. "I had not anticipated the honor of your company. You look particularly lovely tonight."

Erin, suddenly self-conscious, wished the slit on her skirt didn't go up quite so high. "Yeah, these aren't my work clothes," she said.

"Of course not," he said. "I understand thanks are in order, however. You have recovered a priceless work of culture from the hands of a grasping criminal."

"So she can be fought over by more of the same," Erin said, before she could stop herself.

Haddad froze, his mouth slightly open in astonishment. Even Schenk tilted his head to look at her, surprised. Then Haddad threw back his head and laughed. "Well said!" he exclaimed. "And quite true. We shall see which grasping criminal triumphs. It shall be much like a meeting of international politics, with a similar lack of morals. *Herr Doktor* Schenk, welcome. I had not thought to see you here, either. I trust you are recovering well?"

"*Ja*, I am well enough," Schenk said, staring at Haddad as if the other man was something he'd found stuck to the bottom of his shoe. "And you?"

"A mere scratch," Haddad said. "But I am keeping you. Please, enjoy the exhibition. And Miss O'Reilly, if you lack a suitable partner for conversation, or for whatever else you may require, consider me very much at your service."

"You know," she said, "I just might take you up on that."

"I am delighted," he said.

"See, we got the painting," she said. "And we got the thieves. We even got the guy who hired them. But we haven't got the intended buyer yet."

Haddad's face froze.

"But I'm sure it's just a matter of time," she said cheerfully. "After all, I'm sure Van Ormond's gonna sing when the DA lays out the case. How long did you say you'd be in New York?"

"I have urgent business awaiting me at home," he said, recovering a little. "I fear our further acquaintance must await a more opportune time and place."

"Anytime you're in town, I'll look you up," she promised, still managing to keep her tone light and pleasant.

Haddad bowed, a little stiffly, and murmured something to his servant. They moved off.

"Creep," Erin muttered under her breath as he limped away.

"*Ja, Fräulein*," Schenk said. "He is no pleasant man. But you know something about him, *ja*?"

"Yeah," she said. "I'm pretty sure he's Van Ormond's buyer."

"Really," he said. "Why, then, do you not place the handcuffs on him?"

"I can't make arrests. I'm suspended. Anyway, even if Van Ormond talks, we won't be able to make it stick."

"Why is that?"

"No proof," she said. "Haddad's too smart to leave a paper trail. It's his word against Van Ormond's."

"So he gets away with it, as you say?"

"Yeah," Erin sighed. "He does. But he goes home with nothing. I bet I scared him out of New York City for a while. Ten bucks says he flies out tonight, tomorrow morning at the outside."

"I will make no wager with you," he said, smiling. "But he can still purchase the painting at auction, in person or through the Internet."

"Maybe," Erin said. "But he's got to take his chance, like everyone else."

"Like all the other scoundrels," Schenk said. "Look around you. It is like in the old film. All of the usual suspects are, how you say, rounded up. See, there is *Herr* Atkins." He flicked his index finger on the arm of his wheelchair. "He loves women, but cannot keep them. And beside him, arm in arm, Dominique de Vere. She murdered her husband, so they say. *Herr* Atkins should be careful."

"Yeah," Erin said, following Schenk's extended finger. "They were two of my suspects, you know."

"Good choices, *Fräulein*. I almost wish they had stolen her, so that you might arrest them." Schenk smiled coldly. "Who else was on your list?"

"Adlai Martin," she said.

"Ah, *Herr* Martin," Schenk said. "Three wives have left him, all due to his brutish nature. He thinks he loves, but his love, as Dostoevsky writes, is more like hate. See him there, by the punch bowl?"

"The one with the arm candy half his age?" Erin asked, wrinkling her nose.

"*Ja*, that is he," Schenk said. "Another good choice, but I fear he lacks the cunning to be a thief."

"You know who else was on the list?" Erin retorted, growing tired of his self-righteousness. "You."

Schenk was rendered momentarily speechless. Then he chuckled quietly. "Your point is taken, *Fräulein*," he said. "I shall say no more." Then he coughed and doubled over on the wheelchair. Luisa bent over him anxiously. He waved her impatiently back. "Take me to the Madonna, *Fräulein* O'Reilly," he said in a whisper. "And then back to the hospital. I fear my strength is not yet recovered."

*   *   *

The Madonna had been restored to her place of honor in the black velvet-draped gallery. Her serene smile caught Erin and drew her in, just as it had at her first sight of the painting. The blood had been cleaned from her, both new stains and old.

Erin had been raised Catholic. She still wore a silver crucifix around her neck most of the time, especially on duty. But she'd never really appreciated religious art until she'd seen this pure, beautiful portrait. There, in that dark gallery, looking on the holy face of the Virgin as imagined by one of the true masters, she felt a tremor of spiritual awe.

"She's really something, isn't she," a man said just to her left.

"Yeah," she said, and then did a double-take. Luke Devins stood there, hands in the pockets of his tuxedo pants, staring at the Madonna. Erin felt a pang. He hadn't called her since their last conversation in the Priest, and she hadn't called him. But of course he'd be here. They'd left things awkwardly, and he'd been avoiding her. She didn't know whether she was angry or missing him, but he'd left a Luke-shaped hole, and it hurt.

"Luke," she said, then realized she didn't know what to say.

"Erin," he said at almost the same time, turning away from the painting and finally looking her in the face. "I'm sorry. I shouldn't have... I should have..."

"Damn—darn right," she said, glancing at the Madonna. Swearing in the presence of that face was simply impossible. She stepped away, leaving Schenk and Luisa in front of the painting. Luke followed her to a discreet distance. "What was I supposed to think?" she demanded in a harsh whisper. "You left me hanging!"

"I didn't know what to think either," he said. "I had to figure it out, get myself straight, before I could talk to you. Erin, you're amazing. You're one of the toughest women I've ever met, you're smart, you're brave, and you're beautiful."

"But?" she prompted.

"I can't deal with this," he said, his face pained. "Since we've been seeing each other, you've nearly gotten killed twice. The way you work, your job... I can't live that way. I've been losing sleep, wondering all the time if you were okay. Maybe I could get used to it, over time, but I don't think so. There are all kinds of folks who handle it fine. Husbands and wives of cops, firefighters, soldiers. But that's not me. I guess that makes me a coward."

Her anger seeped away. She understood. She thought of her own mother, wondering how Mary O'Reilly had kept herself together for twenty-five years, not knowing whether her husband would come home at the end of his shift. The relief of hearing the familiar footsteps on the stairs, the rush of joy at his safe homecoming, all the time knowing she'd have to go through it all over again the next day, and the next, and the next.

"You're not a coward," she said. "It takes a special kind of faith, and not everybody's got it. It's okay, Luke." And she meant it. It might have been thanks to the Madonna's influence, but she felt serene. The pain and loneliness would come back later, when she was alone again, but for now, she could be gracious. She stepped forward, tilted her head up, and gave him a gentle, lingering kiss, for memory's sake. He returned it. She felt his yearning, the way he moved toward her, and both of them wanted more, but she drew back.

"You're something else, Erin O'Reilly," he said quietly. "I hope you find a guy who deserves you. There aren't many out there. Thank you for finding the Madonna, and for solving the case. I wouldn't... I didn't want Van to get away with it." He looked past her. "Dr. Schenk, I'm glad you could make it. How are you feeling?"

"I live," the German said tersely.

"And congratulations, Doctor," Luke went on.

"For what?" Schenk asked, suddenly suspicious.

Luke blinked, puzzled. "That's why you're here, isn't it? Didn't they tell you?"

"Tell him what?" Erin demanded.

"They're still working on the samples," Luke said. "And the DNA testing takes a while, but the initial blood tests are pretty conclusive. The Association of Art Museum Directors has a set of guidelines for the recovery of Nazi treasure. Their main goal is to restore stolen paintings to their rightful owners. There's some controversy regarding their methodology, but they tend to give the benefit of the doubt to claimants. Dr. Schenk, your uncle... does he have any other living kin?"

"Of his family, I am the last," Schenk said. "Hitler did away with most of us, and the rest have since dwindled."

"That's what I thought," Luke said. "The blood that was on the painting... the lab techs have matched it."

"*Ja*, it is my blood," Schenk said. "I was shot."

"That's not what I meant," Luke said. "The two blood samples matched each other. They've proved the relationship between the two of you. That means the painting is yours."

Schenk sat perfectly still as it hit him. "*Mein Gott*," he murmured. "Can it be?"

"You'll have to wait for them to finish the tests," Luke said. "But they're convinced. Then you just need to file a claim. It may take a while. There'll probably be legal challenges. This is America, after all, Land of Lawsuits. But she'll be yours in the end. Congratulations. You're a millionaire."

"*Nein*," Schenk said, and there were tears in his eyes. "I will not sell her. What do you take me for? It would be like selling my grandmother."

"So what will you do?" Erin asked.

Schenk looked at her. "I will let her rest in the city of the woman who saved her," he said. "As so many of my people did, she has come to America. Here let her remain, one more orphan of that terrible time. She has been hidden from the world long enough."

"There's going to be some pissed-off—I mean, some irritated guys out there," Erin said, pointing a thumb toward the gathered throng of art collectors.

"The vultures?" Luke said, laughing suddenly. "Look on the bright side. They may hate you, but the reporters are going to love this."

"Reporters, ha!" Schenk said. Then he choked. He clapped a hand to his mouth and was wracked with a fit of coughing. When his hand came away, there were flecks of blood on his palm.

"No more," Luisa said with that air of authority that experienced nurses use to order even doctors around. "We go back to the hospital now."

"We have to go," Erin said. "Take care of yourself, Luke."

"You too, Erin," he said, giving her a wistful smile. "I'm... sorry."

"Don't be," she said, mustering up a smile of her own. "You're going to find some nice girl in a nice, safe job and make her very happy."

Chapter 23

Erin's warm serenity lasted until she dropped Schenk and Luisa at the hospital. Alone in her car, she sat in the parking lot for several minutes. When she finally turned the key and the engine started, she responded to the roar of the motor by crashing her fist down on the dashboard. It hurt, but she did it again. Schenk got the painting, Lyons and Spinelli closed their case. What did she get? An ex-boyfriend, a Board of Inquiry, and the very real possibility that she might lose her job and her dog.

She knew it wasn't a good idea to drive angry, but she didn't care. She took out some of her frustration by making hard turns, honking at slow drivers, and stomping the pedals harder than necessary. Still, she made it home without causing any accidents, so it could've been worse.

Erin stormed into her apartment, slamming the door savagely shut behind her. Then she saw Rolf, standing beside the coat closet, tail wagging anxiously. He sensed her foul mood and approached carefully, keeping his head low, tail still sweeping side to side.

Her fit of temper passed, leaving nothing but weariness behind. She kicked off her shoes, stumbled across the room to her love seat, and sprawled out on it. Rolf followed. He watched her for a few moments. Then he picked up one of his chew-toys, returned to her side, and carefully laid it in her lap. He rested his chin on her knee and gave her a deep, brown-eyed stare.

Erin smiled sadly at him. "Thanks, partner," she said. She halfheartedly tossed the toy across the room. Rolf bounded after it, retrieved it, and laid it back on her lap, tail wagging more enthusiastically. They played for a while, and Erin found that her K-9's mood helped lift her own. Eventually, her head cleared enough that she was able to go to bed. She didn't bother to set an alarm. What was the point?

*   *   *

The buzz of her phone woke her. Disoriented, she fumbled for it, seeing the name MURPHY on her caller ID. Wondering what her Lieutenant could possibly want, not yet awake enough to recognize the possibilities; she hit the green answer button just before it could roll to voicemail.

"What is it, Murph?" she asked.

"Oh, good," Murphy replied. "I thought maybe you were dead. Did I wake you?"

"What if you did? I'm on vacation."

"Suspension, O'Reilly. Not vacation. That means I can call you back in. Get dressed and get over here ASAP. Be as presentable as you can."

Now Erin was fully awake, and scared. "Is it the Board?" she asked. "I thought they'd send me a letter or something."

"It's nothing like that," Murphy said. "We've got a guy coming down from Manhattan, a big-shot police captain, wants to see you. Now stop talking and start moving. He'll be here at ten." Her phone beeped and the call ended.

It was just after nine thirty. Erin hardly ever slept in so late. Scolding herself for going soft, she tossed her phone aside and scrambled to find clean clothes that would be suitable for meeting—with whom? A police captain from downtown? What could he possibly want with her? She decided on black slacks and a blue blouse with conservative lines. She ran Rolf out to relieve himself, considered leaving him behind, and said aloud, "The hell with that." He was her partner. They'd face the music together. On a stomach full of nothing but butterflies, avoiding the stares from her fellow officers, she strode into the precinct with much more confidence than she felt.

Murphy was waiting for her in his office with another man. The guy was tall, a clean six-two, and thin. He wore an old-style suit, a Colt Police Special on his hip, and a truly glorious mustache that reminded Erin of Sam Elliott in the movie *Tombstone*. He had a full head of black hair, going gray around the edges. He looked like nothing so much as a Wild West Marshal come to visit the 21st Century.

"Officer O'Reilly?" the stranger said.

"Yes, sir," she said, standing to attention. Rolf mimicked her, sitting straight-backed at her side, ears perked forward.

He smiled. "At ease," he said, extending his hand. "Fenton Holliday. I'm Captain of Precinct 8 up in Manhattan."

She gave him the firmest handshake she could muster. "Good to meet you, Captain. What can I do for you?"

"I understand you're on suspension," Holliday said, "facing a Board of Inquiry regarding interference in an ongoing investigation?"

"That's right, sir," Erin said. She'd been staring straight ahead, avoiding eye contact, but now she glanced into his face. What she saw there surprised her. There was a twinkle in his eye, as if the two of them were sharing a private joke. But if that was the case, the joke was on her. She didn't know where he was going with this.

"You can stop worrying," Holliday said. "The Board has decided not to pursue the matter."

"Really?" Erin exclaimed.

Holliday raised an eyebrow. "Unless you'd rather they continue."

"That's okay," she said quickly. "I just—I don't get it, sir."

"There are two kinds of official inquiries," the captain said. "The kind that stem from gross misconduct, and the kind that are motivated by personal animosity. Would you care to guess which yours was?"

"I think maybe I can," Erin said.

"The Internal Affairs commander in my precinct brought your case to my attention," Holliday continued. "He's not the easiest man to get along with, but he has an eye for good police. You've shown initiative, insight, and the guts to see the job through to the end. He suggested you might be more useful in some other capacity than departmental scapegoat. I happen to agree."

"So where does that leave me?" she asked, bewildered.

"That's up to you," he said. "You can stay here, doing what you've been doing, and keep doing it well. I've looked over your file. You're a good patrol cop. You'll probably make sergeant in a year or two. You can put in your twenty, or twenty-five, and retire with your pension."

"Or?"

"Or you can come to Manhattan and work for me," Holliday said.

"Doing what?"

"I've been asked by the Commissioner's office to set up an auxiliary Major Crimes unit. Manhattan Major Crimes is a little overworked, and they're setting up some new squads. There's an opening, if you're interested. It'll be tough, interesting work. Detective Bureau cases."

"Don't you want detectives for that sort of thing?" she asked.

"Like your friend Spinelli?" Holliday said, raising his eyebrow again. "Lieutenant Webb would be your new CO, and he's a detective, but the rest of the squad came from ESU and Internal Affairs. Someone from Patrol will round it out nicely."

"What about my current partner?"

Holliday blinked. Then he smiled under his mustache. "I'm sorry; I misspoke when I said there was an opening. There are two openings. One for you, and one for your partner, who I hear apprehended an armed suspect only a few days ago. Say the word, and you'll both be transferred to my command in Precinct 8, as soon as we can make it happen."

Erin felt breathless. It seemed like a miracle. Working major cases, in the big city! Getting beyond the day-to-day grind of the patrol beat, Rolf still with her! This was her chance, her shot at doing something extraordinary. She had a dozen, a hundred doubts and fears, but none of them showed in her face or her voice as she looked Captain Holliday straight in the eye.

"I'm honored to serve, Captain."

"Then congratulations, Detective O'Reilly," Holliday said, shaking her hand again. "I'll put the paperwork through. It'll be a few days, so take the rest of the week to get your things in order. I'll expect to see you in Precinct 8 on Monday. You'll be on the second floor. Bring your gun, your shield, and your partner."

"I guess you'll be needing these," Murphy said with a grin, sliding her Glock and shield across his desk.

"Thank you, sir!" Erin said to both of them collectively.

* * *

Erin's euphoria almost overrode her conscious thoughts, but she was already starting to make plans. She'd want to find a place to live closer to her new workplace, and housing in Manhattan was a nightmare. She might have to stay where she was and ride the subway to work. She'd be assigned a different vehicle. Did Precinct 8 have Chargers in their motor pool? She liked the tough, muscular Dodge, but supposed it didn't matter much. What would her new colleagues be like? An ESU door-kicker, a detective, and an IAB cop? What sort of unit *was* this?

But before she did anything else, Erin had a phone call to make. She waited until she was in her car, away from other eyes and ears, and hit her speed dial. The phone rang twice, and then was picked up on the other end. She took a deep breath.

"Hey, Dad? It's me. You'll never guess where I'm going."

Here's a sneak peek from
Book 2: Irish Car Bomb

Coming in 2018

The duty sergeant at the front desk raised an eyebrow. "Help you, ma'am?" he asked.

"I'm looking for Major Crimes," she said.

"And you are?"

"O'Reilly, transfer from Queens 116."

"Okay, sign in," the sergeant said. "Shield?"

She flashed her ID and signed the spiral pad.

"Welcome to the Old Eightball, O'Reilly. You want the second floor." He angled a thumb. "Stairs and elevator."

Riding the elevator to the second floor would be ridiculous. Erin took the stairs.

She and Rolf emerged into a wide-open space. The second floor of the precinct had structural columns dotted throughout. The only walls were around the captain's office, the break room, and the bathroom. She saw a handful of desks with outdated, boxy computer monitors, a whiteboard, a copy machine, a fax, and a meeting table. The table and desks were scarred and scratched. No one was in sight.

"I guess they don't get here early," Erin said. She glanced into the break room. There was a coffee machine, which was good, and a pot of coffee already made up, which was even better, but the couch and coffee table were just about the most disreputable pieces of furniture she'd ever seen.

Her police instincts nagged at her. If a pot of coffee was brewed up, then someone had beaten her here. Where was he, or she?

Even as she thought it, she heard the sound of a faucet from the direction of the bathroom. She turned in time to see Captain Holliday come through the door, drying his hands.

"O'Reilly," he said. "Morning. Glad you're here."

"Thank you, sir," she said, stiffening her spine. "Am I early?"

He smiled through his mustache. "Far from it, Detective. I'm sorry about this, but it looks like you're going to have one of those first days."

"What do you mean, sir?"

"You'll have to learn on the job," he said. "The call from Dispatch beat you here by a quarter of an hour. When the call comes in, the cavalry rides out. You'll have to meet your unit on site."

"We've got a case?" Her heart was suddenly pounding, her jitters forgotten with the rush of excitement that always came when she went into action.

"Apparently a man got blown up on his way to work this morning," the captain said dryly.

"Blown up, sir?"

"Car bomb," Holliday said. "Don't ask me, I wasn't there. You'd best get moving. Call Dispatch. They'll tell you where to go. When you get to the scene, ask for Lieutenant Webb."

Erin hurriedly laid her box of office supplies on the most deserted-looking desk and went straight back outside. Rolf followed.

She'd just gotten out the door of the precinct house and was reaching for a shoulder radio she wasn't wearing when she remembered she didn't have a squad car, either. Mentally kicking herself, she used her phone to call in to Dispatch to get the address. She could've gone back inside and asked Holliday how to access the motor pool, but time was ticking at the crime scene and she was already embarrassed. She'd improvise. The important thing was to get there. She hailed a cab.

*   *   *

The site of the blast was an underground parking garage off Second Avenue, between 24th and 25th Street. Erin paid the cabbie and took in the scene. She was definitely at the right location. Squad cars had cordoned off the garage and a large number of bystanders were milling around at a respectful distance. As she and Rolf approached, she heard a woman say, "I'm sure I saw the bomb squad. Is it terrorists, do you think?"

"Muslims, probably," her companion replied. "Al Qaeda."

Erin inwardly rolled her eyes at the rubberneckers as she passed. The apartment complex was middle-class, about fifteen floors, built of tan bricks with a row of restaurants at ground level. There were no signs of structural damage, no clouds of smoke pouring out of the garage. If this had been a bomb, it hadn't been too big. Going out on a speculative limb, she was willing to bet it didn't indicate a massive terrorist strike on New York City.

She showed her shield to the uniforms at the entrance and identified herself. They stepped aside and she and Rolf went down the ramp. Partway down, the dog abruptly froze in his "alert" posture. A moment later, Erin smelled it too. Rolf was trained in explosives detection, and something had definitely blown up not long before. There was a smell of smoke, burnt fuel, and charred metal.

A small group of men and women were standing around the wreckage of the car. There was a big guy with a broken nose and a blond buzz cut. Next to him was a man in a trench coat, holding an unlit cigarette. A woman with hair dyed electric blue at the tips glanced up, saw Erin, and smiled a little nervously at her. Another woman in a white lab coat was kneeling next to something black and smoldering. The smell told Erin she didn't really want to look closer at it, but figured she'd have to. The last guy was poking around the car. He had a T-shirt emblazoned BOMB SQUAD and a heavy-looking helmet, though it was in his hand instead of on his head.

"Lieutenant Webb?" Erin guessed, looking at the guy in the trench coat.

"That's me," he said. "You must be O'Reilly."

"Yeah," she said. "Sorry I'm late. I went to the precinct first."

Webb shrugged. "Glad you could join us. This is Vic Neshenko," he indicated the big man to his right, who grunted and worked a toothpick from one side of his mouth to the other. "And this is Kira Jones," pointing to the woman with the dyed hair, "and our Medical Examiner, Dr. Sarah Levine," finishing with the lab-coated woman. He didn't introduce the bomb-squad guy.

"Good to meet you," Jones said, offering her hand. Erin shook it, noticing deep crimson fingernails through the translucent glove. "That your dog?"

"Yeah, this is Rolf," she said.

"How long have you had him?"

"We've been partners for three years."

"Okay, great," Neshenko said. "And we've worked together for thirty seconds. Can we look at the dead guy so we can go home?"

Erin leaned forward to peer at the corpse at their feet.

"New girl?" Levine said from below.

"Yeah?"

"Move. You're blocking my light."

"Oh. Sorry." Erin stepped to the side, feeling her face flush. She accidentally elbowed the guy in the T-shirt.

"Hi," he said, extending his hand. "Skip Taylor, Bomb Squad. I'm not in your unit, of course. And don't worry, the device fully activated. There's no further danger. Say, is your dog trained in EOD?"

"Yeah," she said. "But mostly he does suspect tracking and apprehension."

"That's great," Taylor said. "We've got a K-9 in our unit, but he's training this week, counter-terrorist stuff with Homeland Security and the Feebies. But check out this device, this is some great shit. Took our boy clean out of his shoes. Seriously. You see the shoes over there by the car?"

Erin felt a queasy lump in her stomach. "Yeah, I see," she muttered, turning her attention back to her new commanding officer. "Lieutenant, what'd I miss?"

"Not much," Webb said. "We only got here a few minutes ago. The area's been secured, and Taylor's right. There just seems to be the one bomb. It was enough for this guy, though. The uniform who responded didn't even bother calling for the EMTs."

"I can see why," Neshenko said. "Even dental records aren't gonna do much good. It must've gone off right in his face. His head's practically gone."

"Do we know who he is?" Erin asked.

"We think so," Jones replied. "William O'Connell. His wife called it in, said it was their car."

"It's a nice car," Taylor said. "Expensive Audi, maybe three years old. Well, it was. Now it's scrap metal, with a pretty amazing blast pattern."

No one else seemed too eager to indulge Taylor's enthusiasm for explosive mayhem, but Erin figured there had to be some useful information there. "What's amazing about it?"

"Okay, so the device was under the dash and the driver's seat. It's a two-stage blast, which is unusual by itself," he said. "I'm thinking the initial charge was wired to the ignition and went off right under the steering wheel. That set off the secondary, which was a sizable chunk of what I'm guessing was nitro. But what's weird is, he wasn't sitting in the driver's seat when he got blown away."

"How can you tell?" she asked.

"He's over here," the bomb tech explained. "If the charge had gone off under his ass, it would've blown him straight through the roof of the car and he'd have painted the ceiling."

"Nice," Jones muttered.

"Instead, he got tossed this way. That tells me the device went off when he was standing or maybe bending over. I'm guessing he saw something under the dash, maybe spotted some loose wires or even the device itself, and it went off while he was bent over."

"There's some tools over here," Neshenko said, pointing to the garage floor. "I've got a socket wrench, a screwdriver, and what looks like part of a wire cutter, but it's blown to pieces."

"Jesus," Webb said quietly. "You think he found the bomb and tried to defuse it himself?"

"It's possible," Taylor said. "Stupid of him, but possible. Real civvie move."

"Skip, were you in the service?" Erin asked suddenly. The way he talked, the way he carried himself, and his haircut, all reminded her of Paulson, the former Army Ranger she'd worked with back in Queens.

"EOD, two tours in the sandbox," he said. "Came back with all my parts." He held up a hand and wiggled his fingers.

"What kind of idiot finds a bomb in his car and tries to take it apart instead of calling us?" Webb wondered aloud, returning their attention to the shattered body on the concrete.

"The kind who doesn't want cops around, maybe," Neshenko said, kneeling beside Levine, who was still engrossed in studying the corpse. The big detective flipped back the dead man's suit coat to reveal a shoulder holster, a pistol still strapped in it.

"Damn," Jones said. "He was packing."

"Didn't do him any good," Levine said. "Death was instantaneous. COD was blast trauma and shrapnel that penetrated his face, chest, and neck. The right arm has been amputated just below the shoulder and separated from the torso, coming to rest approximately ten meters away from the principal remains. The left hand has been partially amputated, with the second, third, and fifth fingers missing, but once we analyze the blast pattern a little better, we have a good chance of finding..."

"We get the idea," Webb said. "So he was pretty close to the bomb when it went off?"

"He had his hands practically on it," she confirmed.

"She's right," Taylor said. "I saw some wounds like those in Iraq. There was this one kid, he was screwing around with a landmine..." His voice trailed off and his smile faded.

"Okay," Webb said. "So he had a sidearm and was doing something with the bomb, either trying to figure out what it was or trying to defuse it. Sounds like he might have military experience. What else have we got on him?"

"There's a wallet in his hip pocket," Levine said. "It was shielded from the blast by his body, so appears undamaged. There's a rolled-up necktie in his left front pocket and keys in his right front."

"Car keys?" Erin asked.

"Car, house, safe-deposit box," Levine said.

"Well, that proves he didn't set it off by starting the engine," Erin said. "They'd still be in the ignition otherwise."

"Seat belt wasn't fastened either," Taylor said. "Not that that proves anything. If he was dumb enough to monkey with a homemade nitro bomb, he probably wasn't smart enough to buckle up."

"What else have we got from the car?" Webb asked.

"Driver's side door over there," Neshenko said, pointing with his thumb. The door had been blasted away from the car at an angle, leaving a streak of black paint on the garage wall before coming to rest in a twisted heap.

"Yeah, I think the door was open when the bomb went off," Taylor said. "If it was only secured by the hinges, it would've angled forward like that. If it'd been closed, it would've gone in more of a straight line."

"So our victim was leaning over the seat with the door open, standing about where his shoes still are," Webb said.

"Just like car crashes," Erin said, her Patrol experience still fresh in her mind. "You can usually judge point of impact when a pedestrian gets run down by where you find the shoes."

"That's right," Webb said. "Okay, we're getting a picture."

"Trunk's open," Neshenko reported. He was prowling around the edges of the crime scene like a restless junkyard dog. "I got a toolbox, open lid, a triple-A kit, and a spare tire."

"All right," Webb said. "So you're all telling me this guy comes down to the garage, is all set to get into his car, and what? Sees a bomb wired to his ignition switch. For some reason he doesn't call the cops and decides to take care of it himself. Probably because he's a moron. He takes off his tie, stows it in his pants pocket, pops the trunk, opens his toolbox, gets out his tools and tries to take the bomb apart. He screws the pooch, the bomb blows up in his face, and here we are. And there he is."

Erin looked around at the others. All of them were nodding.

"So why doesn't he call the cops?" Erin asked. "Is this guy on the FBI Top Ten? There's nothing illegal in the trunk. Has he got diamonds in the door panels? Cocaine in the glove compartment?"

"We'll go over the car," Taylor said. "I need to confirm the explosive. I'm only guessing it was nitro. I'll know more when I run the lab tests. If there's anything else in there, we'll find it. We're taking the entire vehicle to the department lot."

"We need to talk to the wife," Jones said.

"Where is she?" Erin asked.

"Upstairs, in their apartment," Webb said. "We've got uniforms with her."

"And she's a real piece of work," Neshenko said.

"What do you mean?" she asked.

"You'll see."

Ready for more?

Join Steven Henry's author email list
for the latest on new releases, upcoming books and
series, behind-the-scenes details, events, and more.

Be the first to know about the release of Book 2 in
the Erin O'Reilly Mysteries by signing up at
tinyurl.com/StevenHenryEmail

Acknowledgments

I used to think books were solo operations. But that's not even close to true. There are a large number of people whose time, efforts, and emotional energy have gone into this book. I owe all of them my thanks, and I'd like to list them here.

First off, thank you to Ben Faroe of Clickworks Press, who read this book and liked what he saw. I really appreciate your advice and assistance refining the raw manuscript and cover design. Thank you Ben and Kristen for your hours of careful editing!.

A great big thank you to Kara Salava for the gorgeous photo on the cover and tweaking it to make it perfect. Kristin Salava, you have a handsome beast of a German Shepherd, Kubistraum's All the Right Moves, TC, CGC, TDI, also known as "Bosco". Kelly Foehl, thanks for coordinating your sisters and setting up the photo shoot. And thank you, Bosco, for being a real trooper. Good dog.

Thank you to the Burnsville, MN Police Department and their Citizens' Academy program. You taught me a lot about Patrol work and the life of a police officer. Thank you for teaching me how to do field-sobriety tests, traffic stops, pistol and rifle shooting, and how to take a Taser jolt. You really go out and do what I only write about. Stay safe out there.

Thank you to my first-draft readers: Carl and Mary Caroline Henry, Dave and Marilyn Lindstrom, Kira Woodmansee, and Andrew Peterson. Every writer would like to think our first drafts are good enough to publish. We're always wrong about that. Your feedback, both positive and constructive, made this book better.

This list wouldn't be complete without a shout-out to the PI team. This group of gamers provided the original creative spark for the Erin O'Reilly series. You dreamed up several of the main characters we'll be seeing in later installments. You also gave me the creative spark to build this mirror version of our own world. David Greenfield, Justin Moor, Hilary Alweis, Mark Murphy Jr., Bridget Johnson, and Ben Lurie, you made it possible, and you made it fun.

And last, but certainly not least, I want to thank my lovely wife Ingrid, without whom this book wouldn't exist. You not only came up with the character of Erin O'Reilly, you made her live and breathe for me. You listened to my rough-copy night after night, smoothing out the rough spots. More than that, you've always believed in me more than I can ever quite manage on my own.

About the Author

Steven Henry learned how to read almost before he learned how to walk. Ever since he began reading stories, he wanted to put his own on the page. He lives a very quiet and ordinary life in Minnesota with his wife and dog.

Also by Steven Henry

Ember of Dreams
The Clarion Chronicles, Book One

When magic awakens a long-forgotten folk, a noble lady, a young apprentice, and a solitary blacksmith band together to prevent war and seek understanding between humans and elves.

Lady Kristyn Tremayne – An otherwise unremarkable young lady's open heart and inquisitive mind reveal a hidden world of magic.

Robert Blackford – A humble harp maker's apprentice dreams of being a hero.

Master Gabriel Zane – A master blacksmith's pursuit of perfection leads him to craft an enchanted sword, drawing him out of his isolation and far from his cozy home.

Lord Luthor Carnarvon – A lonely nobleman with a dark past has won the heart of Kristyn's mother, but at what cost?

Readers love *Ember of Dreams*

"*The more I got to know the characters, the more I liked them. The female lead in particular is a treat to accompany on her journey from ordinary to extraordinary.*"

"*The author's deep understanding of his protagonists' motivations and keen eye for psychological detail make Robert and his companions a likable and memorable cast.*"

Learn more at tinyurl.com/emberofdreams.

More great titles from Clickworks Press

www.clickworkspress.com

Hubris Towers: The Complete First Season

Ben Y. Faroe & Bill Hoard

Comedy of manners meets comedy of errors in a new series for fans of Fawlty Towers and P. G. Wodehouse.

"So funny and endearing"

"Had me laughing so hard that I had to put it down to catch my breath"

"Astoundingly, outrageously funny!"

Learn more at clickworkspress.com/hts01.

The Dream World Collective

Ben Y. Faroe

Five friends quit their jobs to chase what they love. Rent looms. Hilarity ensues.

"If you like interesting personalities, hidden depths... and hilarious dialog, this is the book for you."

"a fun, inspiring read—perfect for a sunny summer day."

"a heartwarming, feel-good story"

Learn more at clickworkspress.com/dwc.

Death's Dream Kingdom
Gabriel Blanchard

A young woman of Victorian London has been transformed into a vampire. Can she survive the world of the immortal dead—or perhaps, escape it?

"The wit and humor are as Victorian as the setting... a winsomely vulnerable and tremendously crafted work of art."

"A dramatic, engaging novel which explores themes of death, love, damnation, and redemption."

Learn more at clickworkspress.com/ddk.

Share the love!

Join our microlending team at kiva.org/team/clickworkspress.

Keep in touch!

Join the Clickworks Press email list and get freebies, production updates, special deals, behind-the-scenes sneak peeks, and more.

Sign up today at clickworkspress.com/join.

CPSIA information can be obtained
at www.ICGtesting.com
Printed in the USA
BVHW092347230222
629896BV00002B/254

9 781943 383351